Mills & Boon
Best Seller Romance

A chance to read and collect some of the best-loved novels from Mills & Boon—the world's largest publisher of romantic fiction.

Every month, four titles by favourite Mills & Boon authors will be re-published in the *Best Seller Romance* series.

A list of other titles in the *Best Seller Romance* series can be found at the end of this book.

GW00707914

Anne Mather

TANGLED TAPESTRY

MILLS & BOON LIMITED
LONDON · TORONTO

First published 1969
Australian copyright 1981
Philippine copyright 1981
This edition 1981

© Anne Mather 1969

ISBN 0 263 73724 1

Set in Linotype Baskerville 10 on 11pt.

Made and printed in Great Britain by Richard Clay (The Chaucer Press) Ltd, Bungay, Suffolk

CHAPTER ONE

DEBRA came out of the apartment building into the early warmth of a spring day. The faint mist which shrouded the harbour promised to lift quite soon, and then the magnificent vista from this vantage point would be spread out panoramically below her. When she had learned she was to come to San Francisco on the west coast of the United States she had, at first, been disappointed. She had wanted to see New York and Washington, and all the famous cities crowding the eastern seaboard, but since her arrival here she had forgotten all her earlier misgivings in the satisfying knowledge that she was to live for six months in one of the most beautiful cities in the world. For years poets and writers alike had tried to put into words the beauty of its bays and bridges, clanging street cars, modern skyscrapers and rambling family dwellings, all spreading up and down the almost perpendicular streets of the city. That they had had little success Debra thought was due to the fact that the real thing was so much more warming and exciting and *alive*. In the three months since her arrival she had learned that every street corner could produce an unexpectedly enchanting scene, and below the geographical curve of the peninsula with the silver lance of its bay slicing a cleft through the land mass provided a constant challenge to the artist. She supposed she had fallen in love with the place, and the thought of returning home to England and Aunt Julia filled her with dismay.

Smiling at the friendly mailman who was passing, she began to walk slowly down the steep slope towards the Filbert High School where she was a teacher. She had come from Valleydown in Sussex on an exchange scheme, much to the annoyance of Aunt Julia, her only relative. For some obscure reason Aunt Julia disliked anything to do with America, and besides she had rarely allowed Debra much freedom in England, despite the fact that her niece was now twenty-two and quite capable of taking care of herself. Debra, not wanting to annoy Aunt Julia unnecessarily, had usually fallen in with her wishes. She was not the kind of girl to want to go out a lot, anyway. She loved books, and reading, and classical music, and although her clothes were modern, she was really quite old-fashioned in many ways due of course to Aunt Julia's overpowering influence.

But when this chance had come her way to see something of the world, Debra had determined to take it. After all, there seemed little opportunity of her being able to afford to travel far in the normal course of events. Aunt Julia commandeered most of her salary for housekeeping, and as she knew that Aunt Julia only had a pension to support herself with, Debra did not object. But it meant that she had to make all her own clothes, and it was as well that she used little make-up. Fortunately, her complexion was smooth and creamy, and her eyes, green and slightly tilted at the corners, already had sooty lashes to match her thick dark hair. Although her hair was straight, its length and silkiness required no adornment. In the right clothes, with carefully applied make-up, she could have been quite beautiful, but Debra, engrossed in her small world of books and teaching, was completely unaware of herself.

She swung now round the corner of Maple Vine, and entered the tall gates of the Filbert School. Scarcely above medium height, she looked more like one of the students than their teacher, and sometimes her

6

exuberant pupils took advantage of the fact. But whenever she could she made their lessons so interesting that they forgot to be troublesome. This morning, for example, she had arranged a visit to some television studios, where they were filming a new series of detective stories. The studios were in Market Street, a wide thoroughfare that ran diagonally through the city. At the eastern end of Market Street was the long waterfront which curved past the dozens of piers from where hundreds of ships sailed every month. Debra loved this area; the colourful fishing vessels manned mainly by Italians whose home base was there gave the harbour an almost cosmopolitan appearance, and there was always plenty to see. Sometimes, on Sundays, she took sandwiches for her lunch and spent the whole day browsing about the tiny shops that abounded on the quayside, admiring the tourist stores with their stacks of souvenirs, and sometimes joining a trip that was going out in the bay so that she could look back at the city and imprint it firmly in her memory for when she must return home.

The Filbert School was huge and impressive, but surroundings in educational establishments, thought Debra, were only as good as the teachers within them. After preliminary assemblies, she gathered her class of eighteen and said:

'I've arranged for transport to the studios. Are there any questions you wish to ask before we leave?'

A freckle-faced youth in jeans and a white sweater, with a huge 'F' imprinted upon it, grinned cheekily, and said: 'Will we get to meet any of the stars, Miss Warren?'

Debra shrugged. 'Who knows? I doubt it. We're very small fry, and we've been extremely lucky to be accepted as visitors. The studios are particularly busy, I believe, and of course we won't be expected to over-

7

stay our welcome.'

A girl with a ponytail grimaced. 'Oh, I thought we might be televised ourselves,' she said dejectedly. 'And Ross Madison is there, and we all think he's dreamy, Miss Warren.'

'Oh, Sheralyn!' Debra had to smile. 'This is an educational visit, to demonstrate the techniques of ciné-photography and video-tape recording. Not the annual visit of Ross Madison's fan club!'

There was an outburst of giggling, and Debra relaxed. She would miss this class when she returned to England. Whether it was because most of them came from families in the lower income bracket she wasn't certain, but they seemed to appreciate everything she did for them with exaggerated enthusiasm.

Later they all piled into the coach which was to take them to the studios. The automobile negotiated the steep hills and turns with ease, while Debra sat on the edge of her seat, still a little nervous of the apparent lack of concern displayed by the city's drivers. She was sure that if she could drive she would never dare exceed ten miles an hour down the precarious slopes.

The Omega Studios were large but completely unimpressive outside. It wasn't until they entered the massive reception area which gave on to a flight of stairs leading up to various studios that the full impact of its size and opulence was felt. There were lifts, of course, some of them large enough to carry an elephant should that be necessary, while others were small and self-operable. Several attractive girls were employed as receptionists, used to dealing with every kind of personality from stage, screen and government.

Debra approached the desk, introduced herself, and was put into the charge of a Miss Powell, one of the attractive girls she had noticed at first. The children were staring about them with interest and curiosity, all hoping to see someone of importance. A lift transported them to the tenth floor, where Miss Powell led the way towards one of the larger studios. Debra had a muddled impression of lights and cameras and cables everywhere, before Miss Powell turned to her and said:

'The director here is Emmet Morley. Have you heard of him?'

Debra shook her head. 'I'm afraid not.'

Miss Powell smiled. 'Don't worry. It's not important. Around the studios he's extremely well known, of course. He has directed quite a lot of movies, but your being English makes quite a difference, of course. You may get to meet him. He's a nice man.'

Debra nodded, and they continued with the tour. The children were shown the various cameras used for different shots, the instant video-tape recording machine, and one or two of them even rode on one of the camera dollies. At the moment nothing was happening, but Miss Powell explained that later in the morning some filming would be taking place. The children were fascinated with seeing themselves on the closed-circuit television screens, while from time to time they recognised a familiar face walking across the sets. Much to Sheralyn's and the rest of the girl's disappointment, Ross Madison, the star of the detective series, did not appear, although his leading lady, Marcia Wayne, did, and she signed some autographs before retiring to the control office.

Miss Powell suggested they went along to the restaurant for some coffee, and cokes for the children, and Debra agreed. In the restaurant there were many more familiar faces, and even she recognised a star of his own variety show, Barry Willis. It was around this time that Debra became aware that she was attracting a great deal of attention.

It wasn't so much the fact of being stared at that

troubled her, but rather the sensation of being discussed, rather thoroughly. Some of the older men, who she presumed were camera crews, seemed to find her positively magnetising to look at, and she flushed with embarrassment and said to Miss Powell:

'Is it my imagination, or are all these people staring at me?'

Miss Powell glanced around. She shrugged. 'I'm not sure. Why?'

Debra sighed. 'I'm sorry, I don't want to sound ridiculous. It's just a feeling I have. Maybe they don't see parties of children and their teacher visiting the studios every day.'

Miss Powell laughed. 'Heavens, there are frequently visitors coming round. I think you're probably imagining it.' She looked critically at Debra. 'You're a very attractive girl. Has no one ever told you so?'

'Oh, heavens, no!' Debra felt worse than ever.

Miss Powell narrowed her eyes. 'Are there no men in England? Or do you live in a convent there?'

Debra twisted her fingers together. 'Not at all. It's just that I don't have much time ... for that sort of thing.'

'I thought London was the swingingest city in the world,' remarked Miss Powell mockingly.

'Valleydown, where I live, is thirty miles from London,' returned Debra swiftly. 'Anyway, this is hardly the kind of conversation we should be having. Will we be returning to the studios?'

Miss Powell smiled and accepted the rebuff with good grace. 'Yes,' she said, 'we'll go back. I promised Mr. Morley that the children should see a little of the actual shooting going on.'

Back in studio seven, Emmet Morley was already on the set giving final instructions to his cast. When the sound of the children entering came to his ears, he came over, smiling expansively, a huge cigar hanging from his mouth. Debra looked at him with interest. He was the first director she had seen, and the fact that he had directed films pointed to his being more important than she had imagined. He was of medium height and veering to plumpness, but he had a charming smile, and used it to good effect. He grinned at Miss Powell, said, 'Hi, Lucy,' and then looked at Debra.

At once his expression changed. His amiable approach gave way to a disbelieving glare, and something like recognition flickered in his small eyes. He swept the cigar out of his mouth and narrowed his lids, then ran a hand over his forehead, up to the receding line of his hair. Then he said:

'Your name. What's your name?'

Debra was taken aback, and glanced desperately at Lucy Powell. But Lucy merely looked surprised too, and Debra answered: 'Debra Warren, Mr. Morley.'

He studied her appraisingly, replacing the cigar in his mouth and gnawing at it abstractedly. The children were staring too, now, all wondering what was going to happen, and hoping for some excitement. Debra felt terrible. In the restaurant she had felt as though she was being stared at, but this—this was much worse. Why on earth did Emmet Morley stare at her like that, and why didn't he hurry up and say something and get it over with? The whole studio seemed conscious of the small scene being enacted just inside the wide doors, and a strange hush had descended.

Lucy Powell eventually broke the silence by saying: 'This is the schoolteacher from Filbert, Mr. Morley. The English girl who is over here on the exchange scheme.'

Morley drew heavily on his cigar, gathered his thoughts, and lifting his shoulders in a helpless gesture, said: 'Yeah, the English teacher from the High School.' He glanced round thoughtfully. 'Go on looking around, kids! Lucy, do me a small favour, will you? Take charge of these kids for five minutes. Give me a moment to speak to Miss ... er ... Warren, in private.'

Lucy looked taken aback, and not particularly pleased. 'Mr. Morley, I have other visitors to show round after this party has left——' But she was left talking to herself, for ignoring her protests, Emmet Morley had determinedly taken Debra's arm, and was propelling her across the studio floor, past the interested eyes of the camera men, to a small office at the back of the studio. Debra herself tried to protest, but Morley merely said:

'Relax, kid, relax! No one's going to frighten you. I only want to have a small talk with you. Right?'

'I suppose so.' Debra could hardly refuse without causing an embarrassing scene. Besides, what could happen to her? The office was glass-panelled, and all eyes would be on them, anyway.

The office held a couple of easy armchairs, a low desk and several telephones. Emmet Morley seated himself behind the desk and waved to one of the armchairs. 'Sit down, for heaven's sake. I'm not going to eat you! You look positively petrified!'

'Well, quite frankly, I am rather nervous,' she said, subsiding on to an armchair, and then seeing that by doing so she was out of sight of the rest of the studio because the glass panelling only started some three feet from the floor, standing up again.

'You've no reason to be so,' remarked Morley impatiently. 'Good God! Sit down. What on earth experience has made you act like this? Did some guy attack you, or something?'

Debra stiffened her shoulders. 'Of course not. It's

merely that all this is beyond me, and I wish it were over and done with. I can't think what we have to say to one another. Everybody is staring at me as though I were a freak or something! Do I look like a freak?'

Morley's hard features relaxed into a smile. 'Anything but! You're a particularly attractive girl. Surely you know that without me telling you? Sure you do. Even a girl like you couldn't be so dumb!'

'And is that all this is about?' exclaimed Debra disbelievingly.

Morley hesitated. 'More or less,' he muttered evasively. 'Now, will you sit down?'

Debra did so unwillingly, and accepted a cigarette from the box he offered to her. After it was lit, Emmet Morley studied her silently for a while before saying:

'What part of England do you come from, Miss Warren?'

Debra shrugged. 'I don't suppose you'd have heard of it. It's a place called Valleydown, in Sussex. It's actually about thirty miles from London.'

'I see. And your parents? Do you live with them?'

'No. My parents are dead.'

Emmet Morley leaned forward interestedly. 'Is that so? How did they die?'

Debra frowned. 'I don't see what that has to do with anything.'

'Just answer the question, Miss Warren,' muttered Morley impatiently.

Debra compressed her lips in annoyance. What right had this man to speak to her so peremptorily? But she still answered him, albeit a little sulkily. 'They were killed. In a train crash. When I was just a baby.'

'So? Go on, who brought you up?'

'You want my life history, Mr. Morley?'

'More or less, Miss Warren. Go on ... *please*.'

Debra sighed. 'I was brought up by my aunt, Aunt

Julia, that is.'

'I see.' He lay back in his chair. 'Tell me, kid, what do you know about Elizabeth Steel?'

'Elizabeth Steel?' Debra shook her head. 'Why, hardly anything. I mean, I know she was very famous, and that she was killed in a plane crash, but that's about all. Why?'

Morley did not answer her. Instead he said: 'She was famous, *very* famous, as you say. And very popular, too, if a little conceited sometimes. Her death was a tragedy for us all. She was only forty-three, and no one could have guessed even that. She was at the peak of her career.' He sighed heavily. 'That happened a little over ten years ago, when you'd have been—how old?'

Debra thought for a moment. 'Twelve, I suppose.'

'Hmn! Interesting, very interesting.' Morley's eyes were uncomfortably intent.

Debra lifted her shoulders. 'Mr. Morley, what is all this about? I mean, you invite me in here, you want to know my life history and now you start asking me about some film star who's been dead over ten years! I mean, it just doesn't add up. I'm sorry this Steel woman is dead, of course. But I don't see what I have to do with any of it.'

Emmet Morley stubbed out his cigar. 'Okay, okay, Miss Warren. Don't blow your top. We'll leave it—for now at any rate. Just out of interest, do you remember your parents?'

Debra frowned. 'Not at all. Why?' She sounded distraite.

Morley shrugged. 'Cool it, Miss Warren,' he advised her sardonically. 'I have my reasons, believe me, for this interrogation. But I don't think it would be fair at this time to voice them. I'm sorry, kid, but there it is.'

Debra stood up and walked to the door. 'Can I go now?'

'I guess,' he replied laconically, and standing up as well followed her out of the office and across the studio floor again to where Lucy Powell was waiting with the children. She looked bored and impatient, and relinquished her charges with some relief. Then, as Debra was about to suggest it was time to leave, Emmet Morley said:

'Say, you kids, how'd you like to see your Miss Warren take a screen test?'

Debra turned to him, compressing her lips angrily. 'Oh, really——'

'We sure would!' exclaimed Pete Lindsay, her freckle-faced pupil.

'That's for sure!' echoed the others.

'Go on, Miss Warren, be a dare-devil!'

'They may make you a television star,' exclaimed Sheralyn dreamily. 'Oh, Miss Warren, fancy working with Ross Madison!'

All the children were enthusiastic, seeing this as an excuse to stay away from school a bit longer. Debra herself was convinced Emmet Morley had deliberately appealed to the children on her behalf because he knew she would have refused had they been alone. As it was, she felt she would look small and petty if she refused. And also she was sure that this was what Morley had wanted all along, but like the shrewd man he was, he had waited until the perfect opportunity presented itself so that she could not refuse.

'Mr. Morley,' she began slowly, 'I really think it's time we were leaving. I'm sorry, but——'

'Nonsense!' exclaimed Emmet Morley, his faint frown an indication that she was annoying him too. 'What are you so scared of here, Miss Warren? We're not monsters, we're only human beings, the same as everyone else.'

'I . . . I'm not scared!' exclaimed Debra furiously.

'Then what have you to lose? Take the test!'

Debra clenched her fists. 'You're ... you're making it practically impossible for me to refuse.' She glanced round at the children. 'You know perfectly well that if I do refuse it will seem churlish. Besides disappointing the children!'

'Exactly. So what are we hanging about for?' he remarked dryly.

Debra's eyes met his for a moment, and then she capitulated. 'Oh, very well. But I still think it's all rather ridiculous!'

Lucy Powell, who had been standing close by listening, moved nearer to Debra as Morley walked away to arrange for the test. She gave Debra a studied glance, and then said: 'What gives? Are you some relation of his?'

'Of course not,' exclaimed Debra, rather shortly, and then added contritely: 'I've no idea what's going on. Do many people take tests?'

'A fair number. But not like this, straight off the cuff, so to speak. There are always hundreds of people, men and women, all hanging around waiting to get "discovered" as they say. But in your case you have the satisfaction of knowing that what's happening to you is practically a unique experience.'

'But why?'

'That's what I'd like to know. I've never known Morley interest himself in unknowns before, except when he expects to make a deal of money out of it.'

Debra sighed weakly. 'It's fantastic! Oh, well, I hope it's soon over.'

'Pray that it's a success,' remarked Lucy sardonically. 'Have you any idea what you could earn as a television personality?'

'Money doesn't interest me,' exclaimed Debra. 'At least, only so far as keeping me in food and clothes is concerned. I've no aspirations to grandeur.'

'Amazing,' remarked Lucy dryly, and walked away, leaving Debra to her own confused thoughts.

In the shortest space of time the studio was cleared and Morley took charge. Debra was amazed at the way he shed his semi-indolent manner and became a veritable tiger when his wishes weren't carried out instantly. She glimpsed the genius behind the façade and was suitably impressed. The cast of the series were not particularly pleased to be shifted off the set, and Debra felt awful about the whole business. It just wasn't feasible that Emmet Morley was doing all this because he liked her face, and the reasons hidden were beginning to trouble her.

But when it came to the actual test she found it was not at all difficult, after all. She followed his instructions implicitly, and found that once she was actually before the cameras her nervousness fled and she relaxed completely. She didn't know why, but she felt an affinity with the artificial scenery, the set of a comfortable lounge, and in consequence when she was handed a script she read from it without actually thinking about it. She had always been good at amateur dramatics, and had taken part in several school plays, but even she was unaware that she was particularly good until at the end of her speech the whole studio resounded with the applause of the watching crew.

Hot, flushed and embarrassed, she thrust the script back into Morley's hand and said:

'Please, now can I go?'

Morley seemed abstracted, and merely nodded, as though lost in his own thoughts, and Debra made good her escape. She didn't know why she had this incredible urge to get away, but it was overpowering, and she breathed a sigh of relief when the studio doors swung

17

to behind them.

The children were admiring and loud in their praise, but Debra managed to quieten them. She had no particular wish to remember what had just occurred. She was no stage-struck teenager, and all she could feel was relief that her ordeal was over. She refused to consider what might be behind it all. It had been a strange experience, and she felt uncomfortably suspicious that Emmet Morley would not let her get away so easily. It would be an easy matter for him to find her telephone number if he wanted to get in touch with her.

She shook these thoughts away impatiently. It was no good worrying over something that might never happen. She straightened her shoulders. After all, she would not allow herself to be bulldozed into anything she did not like.

It wasn't until she was in bed that night and musing over the day's events that she recalled the words she had spoken during her screen test. Emmet had thrust the script into her hand and she had been too bemused to register what it was. But now she remembered: it had been 'Avenida' and the words she had spoken were Laura's words; Laura, the part which had given Elizabeth Steel her greatest success.

CHAPTER TWO

DEBRA poured herself a cup of coffee and carried it through to the wide window seat in the lounge. From here she had an uninterrupted view of the outer waters of the harbour, and at this hour of the early evening it was unbelievably beautiful. The apartment was small, and not always quiet as it was now, the rest of the building being taken up by young people who seemed to spend their nights playing records and dancing, despite the complaints of the landlady downstairs, but the situation made up to Debra for everything else it lacked. She spent hours sitting here, sometimes sketching idly, and sometimes just dreaming, and remembering that in twelve short weeks she would be back in Valleydown.

The prospect of returning to her aunt's house was not an inviting one. Aunt Julia was not a gregarious person, and did not welcome company in the small house backing on to the river. She was content to sit and knit, and watch television, and sometimes read a magazine. She did a little gardening, complained about the neighbours and the housework, and the cost of groceries, and this was her whole world. In truth Debra had begun to think it was hers too. But this trip had been a revelation in more ways than one. She had met so many people, nice people, who were genuinely interested in her. Back home in England, any friendships she had made were quickly snuffed by Aunt Julia, and Debra had been loath to bring friends to her aunt's house after Aunt Julia had been rude to a fellow teacher from the school.

She had never had a regular boy-friend. She had

occasionally attended lectures together with fellow teachers, some of whom happened to be men, but this was all.

But here, in America, everything was different. There was no Aunt Julia to prevent her making friends, and only the habits of years curtailed her social activities. She was still very shy, and it was difficult to respond naturally to the natural exuberance of her colleagues. And yet she knew that given more time, it would come, if only she had the chance.

She sighed, and lit a cigarette. She didn't smoke a lot, not at all at home, but she enjoyed a cigarette with a cup of coffee at this hour of the evening. She wondered idly what her life would have been like if her parents had lived. She didn't know much about them. As long as she could remember there had only been Aunt Julia, and Valleydown. She could vaguely remember living somewhere else, somewhere nearer London, but always with Aunt Julia. Whenever she questioned her aunt about her parents she received no satisfactory answers. Julia seemed to think the fact that they had both died in a train crash was sufficient to tell a lonely child, not understanding that Debra would have cherished every memory she could relate with avid attention.

Debra shrugged these thoughts away as being disloyal. After all, had it not been for Aunt Julia she would have been in a children's home, and Aunt Julia had described them in terrible terms, whenever she wanted to frighten Debra into submission for some misdoing.

Footsteps on the stairs outside the apartment, loud and frequent, heralded the arrival home of the three boys who lived in the flat above her. A few minutes later the throbbing beat of a current pop song came clearly from above, and Debra sighed again, and standing up walked back into the tiny alcove which served as a kitchen, and replaced her cup on the draining board.

It was only a little after seven-thirty, and the evening stretched ahead of her. She wondered what she would do. She didn't much like to go out alone, and she had made no arrangements to meet any of the girls from the High School this evening. She supposed she could go to the movies, but on an evening like this the prospect did not appeal.

Suddenly the telephone rang shrilly, and Debra almost jumped out of her skin. She was still not used to the ubiquitous presence of the telephone, and in consequence usually felt her nerves jangle when its bell broke the quietude of her thoughts. Stubbing out her cigarette, and wondering who could be calling her, she lifted the receiver.

'Yes,' she said. 'Debra Warren speaking.'

An unfamiliar male voice came to her ears. 'Miss Warren? Good? I understand you took a party of teenagers to the Omega studios a couple of days ago.'

Debra pressed a hand to her stomach. She had still not quite recovered from that, to her, unpleasant sensation of being thoroughly appraised, and although she had thrust it to the back of her mind, at the man's words it all came flooding back.

'That's right,' she said, her voice cool. 'But I must warn you that I have absolutely no interest in any further screen tests or auditions, or anything like that. I'm a schoolteacher, and I have no desire to be a film star!'

The man made a sound which seemed like suppressed humour, and Debra gripped the receiver tightly.

'Please,' she said. 'Whoever you are, get off this line!'

'Hold on, hold on,' he said hastily. 'Look, my name is Dominic McGill, and I want to see you.'

Dominic McGill! Debra's brain buzzed chaotically. Dominic McGill! She knew that name! Who was he? A film star? No! Her brain rejected this. Where had she seen his name? *Recently*! She ran a hand over her forehead puzzlingly.

'I'm a playwright,' he supplied, as though reading her thoughts.

Of course! Debra's memory clicked. Dominic McGill, the playwright! That was where she had seen his name—on the script that Emmet Morley had given her to read. Dominic McGill had written 'Avenida', the play that when filmed had given Elizabeth Steel her most successful role!

Swallowing hard, she said: 'I really can't imagine why you're ringing me, Mr. McGill.'

'Can't you? Well, maybe not, at that. Anyway, that changes nothing. I still want to see you.'

'And I've explained I want nothing more to do with that screen test,' said Debra quickly. 'Look, understand me, Mr. McGill, I'm not some stage-struck teenager. Whatever you have to say doesn't interest me one bit!'

'Is that so?' He sounded rather less amicable now. 'Now, you *look*, Miss Warren! I have no intention of discussing this matter over the phone. When will it be convenient for me to come round?'

'To come round?' echoed Debra in amazement. 'Surely I can't make it any plainer. I don't want to have anything more to do with it!'

'Miss Warren,' his voice was cold now, and for some reason she shivered, 'I mean to see you. Now tell me when, like a good girl!'

'Don't patronise me,' she said angrily. 'For goodness' sake! There ought to be laws against this sort of thing.

22

I'm going to hang up now, Mr. McGill. Please don't ring again!'

And she did so, slamming down the phone with a sense of satisfaction, a malicious kind of satisfaction which she didn't know she possessed.

Then she lit herself another cigarette, and switched on her television, turning the volume up high to drown the wailing tones of the guitars in the flat above. She was annoyed to find herself trembling, and she shook herself violently. Why had she this awful feeling of apprehension suddenly? Just because a producer had taken a fancy to her and had her tested, it didn't mean that she was no longer in control of her own destiny. And Dominic McGill! She shrugged bewilderedly. Imagine receiving a call from Dominic McGill! It was all quite fantastic, and quite crazy.

She crossed to the mirror and studied her face seriously for a minute. What was there there to attract such interest? She wasn't particularly beautiful. Since arriving in San Francisco she had seen dozens of beautiful girls, with much more clothes sense than she had. Besides, surely the fact that she herself wasn't interested would be enough to put them off.

She grimaced at herself mockingly, and then picking up the book she was reading, she subsided on to the couch, completely ignoring the television.

About an hour later her doorbell rang. Frowning, she put down her book and glanced at her watch. It was almost nine. Immediately she felt nervous. Who could be calling on her at this hour? She crossed to the door, and without unfastening the bolt, she opened it to the width of the chain catch.

A man stood outside. He was tall, very lean and tanned, as though he spent long hours in the open air, with hair of that particular shade of ash-blond as to appear silvery in some lights. He was not handsome;

his features were hard and craggy, but he had very light blue eyes, fringed by dark lashes, that seemed to penetrate Debra with their intensity, and she felt a shaky feeling assail her lower limbs.

'Y . . . yes?' she said, keeping half behind the door.

'I'm Dominic McGill,' he said, in a quiet voice. 'Can I come in?'

Debra's fingers tightened on the door handle. 'No,' she said, trying to keep her voice steady. 'We . . . we said all we had to say over the phone.'

'No,' he shook his head, 'We didn't. Now, open the door.'

His voice was still quiet, but his blue eyes had narrowed and Debra felt suddenly afraid. After all, who did she really know here, in San Francisco? A few teachers at the High School. Her landlady? Who would miss her if she disappeared?

'Please,' she said, running a tongue over her dry lips, 'go away. I . . . I don't want anything to do with it. I'm sorry if you've had a wasted journey.'

'Open the door,' he repeated, ignoring her pleas.

Debra closed her eyes momentarily. 'And if I don't?'

'You will.'

She glanced back at the telephone. 'I could call the police.'

'You could be dead before they arrive,' he remarked, as though he was discussing the weather.

'Oh!' Debra pressed a hand to her mouth.

'Oh, for God's sake, open the door,' he said coldly. 'You have nothing to fear from me.'

Debra unlatched the door with shaking fingers, unable to resist any longer. She opened it wider, and he stepped inside, into the light. Then, as before with Emmet Morley, she saw his sudden shock of recognition, before he controlled his expression.

She saw now he was a man in his late thirties,

dressed casually in a turtle-necked navy blue sweater over grey pants, a grey car-coat over all. She thought he was very attractive, and stifled the idea. But there was a kind of animal magnetism about him that was hard to ignore. Whatever kind of life he had led, it had not been always easy, she thought. He was no soft-skinned drone; and this was part of his attraction. He would not be a man to play around with—in any way.

'So,' he murmured, 'you are Debra Warren.'

Debra did not reply, but merely stood there rubbing her elbows with the palms of her hands nervously.

'Emmet tells me you made a good test. And you read part of Laura's script from "Avenida".'

Debra shrugged and nodded.

'Tell me,' he said, 'are your parents living?'

Debra shook her head. 'No.'

'Don't give too much away,' he remarked dryly, lighting himself a cigarette. 'Who were they?'

'I never knew them. I . . . I suppose my father was my aunt's brother, as our names are the same.'

He studied her thoughtfully. 'And you never knew Elizabeth Steel.'

Debra stared at him exasperatedly. 'Oh, not that again!' she exclaimed. 'How would I know Elizabeth Steel?'

He ignored her question and said: 'Where do you live?'

'Didn't Mr. Morley tell you?' she asked sarcastically.

'Yes. But you tell me.'

Debra exhaled irritably. 'Valleydown, in Sussex. Don't tell me you've heard of it!'

Again he ignored her outburst, much to her annoyance.

'How old were you when they died?'

Debra compressed her lips. 'I don't know.'

'Come on. When?'

Debra squared her shoulders. 'Now look here,' she said. 'You've come here, practically forced your way in and asked a lot of questions for which you've received answers. Now this is all! Do you understand?' Her green eyes were blazing, and he seemed lost in some speculative study. Then he shrugged, his eyes cold.

'You look here,' he said, in a quiet voice that emanated suppressed violence. 'Sure I've come here uninvited, sure I've asked you questions, and can you say in all honesty you don't know what in *hell* I'm talking about?'

'Of course I can!' Debra felt something suspiciously like tears behind her eyes, pricking uncomfortably. 'If I knew what it was all about, maybe I'd be able to tell you what you want to know. Because it seems obvious to me that you want something that at present you're not getting.'

'You're damn right,' he muttered, his blue eyes piercing her cruelly. 'I really believe you're on the level!'

Debra was breathing swiftly. 'For goodness' sake,' she exclaimed, 'get to the point!'

'All right, all right, I will!' He flung his cigarette out of the half-open window, staring momentarily on the midnight blue scene below him, lit like stars with the myriads of lights of the city.

Then he looked back at her. 'All right, Miss Warren. You can have it straight. Elizabeth Steel may have been your *mother*!'

For a moment there was silence in the apartment, and then Debra gave a nervous laugh. 'You must be joking,' she exclaimed.

He shook his head, and said: 'Say, do you have anything to drink around here?'

Debra shook her head. 'Only Coke.'

He smiled sardonically, and for a brief moment she

could not drag her eyes away from him. Then she hunched her shoulders and looked towards the kitchen. 'Do you want some coffee?'

He shrugged, and then tucked his fingers into the back waistband of his trousers, walking across to the television, and switching it off firmly. 'Now,' he said, 'let's have some conversation. What do you really know about your parents?'

Debra twisted her fingers together. 'Before you start asking questions, let me ask one,' she said. 'Why are you so sure I might be Elizabeth Steel's daughter? Where's the connection?'

He put his hand into his inside pocket and drew out a wallet. From it he extracted a photograph which he handed silently to Debra. She stared at it in amazement. She might have been looking at a photograph of herself. But this woman's face was older more mature, and yet, basically, there was little difference. The hair, the eyes, the whole expression, was emphatically identical.

'I see,' said Debra, breathing shakily. 'Now I understand.' Then she looked up at him. 'Even so, it's possible for anyone to have a double.'

He lit another cigarette before answering. 'Sure it is, and that's why Emmet wanted to test you. I guess he thought that if you were conceivably some relation of Steel's it would show.'

'And?'

'Well, let's say the resemblance was sufficient to warrant further investigation.'

Debra brushed back her hair from her eyes, feeling bewildered. It was like some crazy dream, brought about by the disturbing affair at the studios. This couldn't actually be happening to *her*. Her parents had been English, they had been killed in a train crash when she was a baby. She could not possibly be Elizabeth Steel's daughter.

'This is ridiculous,' she said unsteadily. 'My parents died in a train crash years ago. If I was Elizabeth Steel's daughter why was I brought up in England? And who is Aunt Julia?'

Dominic McGill put the photograph back in his wallet, then he said: 'Elizabeth Steel was English, even though she made her greatest impact professionally in the States. It's quite possible that your aunt—did she bring you up, by the way?' and at her nod, he continued:—'it's possible that your aunt was Elizabeth's sister—or I should say *is* her sister.'

'That sounds unlikely.'

'I agree. It is unlikely, but I find in this business the unlikeliest things *can* happen.' He looked at her thoughtfully. 'What are you thinking? That you wish you'd never gone to the Omega studios?'

'How did you guess?' Debra managed a small smile.

'But why? For most girls it would be a dream come true?'

'If it is true, why didn't Elizabeth Steel bring me up herself? And why have I never heard of her from Aunt Julia?'

Dominic McGill shook his head. 'I can't tell you that. Not at the moment, anyway. Her producer, Aaron Johannson, knew her longest. He might know. Unfortunately he's out of the country at the moment, filming on location in Spain. But when he comes back . . .'

'Mr. McGill,' Debra chose her words carefully, 'even if it's true, that I am Elizabeth Steel's daughter, what then? What will it achieve to know the truth?'

'Look, Miss Warren, when Steel died she left a small fortune. She had no apparent next of kin. The money is in trust.'

Debra shook her head slowly. 'I don't want the

money.' She shivered. 'If that's the whole point of this enquiry, then forget it. I have enough money for my needs.'

Dominic McGill looked exasperated. 'Oh, don't give me that,' he said, raising his eyes heavenward. 'Look! Okay, I guess the knowledge that your mother may have abandoned you at birth isn't pleasant hearing, but at least have the sense to realise that if there is any money it's yours to use as you like.' He drew deeply on his cigarette. 'Besides, that's not all. Aaron is on the point of remaking "Avenida". Can you imagine the impact you would make in that part?'

'Me?' Debra looked astonished. 'I can't act!'

'Anybody can be a film star,' replied Dominic McGill laconically. 'They're not all Oliviers, you know.'

'Does it occur to you that in spite of all this I may be happy as I am?'

McGill's eyes were derisive. 'You really are quite a girl, aren't you?' he mocked her. 'The only woman I've ever met who is actually not curious! Do you mean to tell me you can go back to—what was it—Valleydown, and forget everything I've told you? Won't it ever trouble you that I might *just* be right?'

Debra turned away. She couldn't take it in. She couldn't be Elizabeth Steel's daughter. She just *couldn't*. But as she tried to find some truth in all that she had been told certain things came back to her; her aunt's refusal to discuss her parents; the pathetically little she knew about them; and most of all, Aunt Julia's hatred of all things American.

She turned back to McGill. 'So,' she said, 'if I do accept all that you've told me, what then?'

Dominic McGill's eyes narrowed. 'Well, now, I guess we wait until Aaron comes home. And then it's up to you. Can you dismiss it all?'

Debra felt the hot tears pricking at her eyes. 'You know I can't,' she cried tremulously. 'Oh, why did you have to come here, why did I ever arrange that visit to the studios?'

'The astrologers would likely call it fate,' he remarked lazily. 'Calm down, kid, it's not the end of the world. It may be the beginning of yours.'

'I *was* happy, I was,' she cried, staring at him with wide eyes. 'You'll never believe me, I know, but I'm not cut out for this sort of thing. I never wanted to be anything than what I am!'

'A schoolteacher!'

'Don't say it like that. I like working with children.'

'You don't look much more than a kid yourself,' he said.

'I'm twenty-two,' she replied indignantly.

'A great age,' he remarked sardonically. 'Oh, to be twenty-two again!'

'I'm sure you don't mean that.'

'You're right. But even at twenty-two, I didn't have that dewy-eyed innocence. God, if Steel was your mother you've a hell of a lot to learn.'

He walked to the door. 'Tomorrow's Saturday. I guess you won't be working.'

'I . . . I have a baseball match to attend in the afternoon,' she said quickly.

'High livin',' he mocked, his expression amused. 'Okay, make it Sunday. At least that will give you a couple of days to cool down. I'll pick you up at eleven in the morning, right?'

'Why?' Debra stared at him.

'I have something to show you,' he replied casually, opening the door. 'Don't worry, honey. You may find something in all this to enjoy.'

'But——' Debra linked her fingers. 'I'm sure there ought to be something more than this to say. I mean, how do I know you are who you say you are?'

He grinned then, a completely charming relaxation of his features. 'Honey, no one would dare to impersonate *me*!'

Then he closed the door behind him, leaving her alone with her thoughts. She ran to the door, but as her fingers closed over the handle she found she could not turn it. It was no use calling him back. It was her problem, and no one else's, and her heartache if it turned out to be true. What kind of a person was Elizabeth Steel to turn her back on her own baby? Had she never had any curiosity about her own child? Did she have no desire to see her, developing into a child, and then ... But her thoughts were brought up short. Elizabeth had been killed when she was only twelve years old. Might she have changed if she had lived? Would she eventually have acknowledged her offspring?

And on the heels of this thought came another: if Elizabeth Steel was her mother, who was her father? Was she *illegitimate*? Was that why so little interest had been taken in her? Oh, God, she thought, feeling sickened. 'It couldn't be true,' she said aloud, as though by voicing the opinion, it negated it.

But the fact remained that there was a faint, yet sturdy, vein of authenticity about the whole affair. So many things linked together, most particularly her aunt's attitude.

And yet why should her aunt act that way? Why pretend she had no mother, even if that mother refused to acknowledge her? There were hundreds of children in similar circumstances, living with relatives because their parents hadn't time for them. It didn't make sense.

When she went to bed that night her thoughts were no further forward. She felt a healthy resentment to-

31

wards Dominic McGill for coming here so arrogantly, and brutally destroying her peace of mind. She was also aware that she had never met a man like him before. He could be hard and cold, yet when he smiled he had the charm of a small boy. A man of moods and complexities, completely outside her comprehension.

She rolled over in her bed, punching her pillow into shape angrily. Whatever came of all this, whatever truths were uncovered, Dominic McGill was merely interested in her as Elizabeth Steel's daughter, and as such, a possible asset to the remake of his famous 'Avenida'. She must *never*, at any time, start thinking of him as a friend of hers.

CHAPTER THREE

On Saturday afternoon at the baseball game, Debra was surprised to be approached by David Hollister, the school principal. Hollister, a man in his early forties, was a bachelor, and had taken a friendly interest in Debra's career since her arrival at Filbert. He had made her feel welcome, and was more than willing to listen to any problem she might encounter.

Debra, used to the stiff formality of an English headmistress, had been astonished when the principal addressed her as Debra from the start, and introduced himself as David. In consequence, although she liked talking to him, she had been inclined to aloofness, unable to wholly lose her normal detachment when speaking to him.

Today, however, after yesterday's revelations which had cost her a night's sleep already, she was more relaxed, and she smiled when he said:

'I think you're beginning to like our national sport.'

'I am,' she agreed, nodding. 'Particularly when our side is winning. Pete Lindsay is in my class.'

'Of course he is,' said the principal reflectively. 'But tell me, Debra, what is all this about the Omega Studios, and Dominic McGill?'

Debra was taken aback. 'You ... you know?' she exclaimed.

'Of course. How do you imagine they got your telephone number?'

'Well, from the book, I suppose,' murmured Debra awkwardly. 'You mean they rang you?'

'Exactly. It was obviously the most satisfactory way.

33

But anyway, enough of that, what exactly did he have to say to you? Or is it too private for me to know?'

'Oh, no—that is—well, actually, what did they tell you?'

'Dominic McGill rang me. He told me he wanted to get in touch with you. Something about a screen test at the studios. Was that in the itinerary, by the way?'

'Of course not.' Debra was blushing furiously. 'You must think me a stage-struck teenager!'

David Hollister gave a short, mirthless laugh. 'Hardly that, my dear, but I must confess I was disturbed when I found that a member of my staff had been taking a screen test.'

'I was practically forced into it,' replied Debra quickly. 'Mr. Morley, Emmet Morley, that is, one of the directors——'

'I have heard of Emmet Morley,' remarked Hollister dryly.

'—well, Mr. Morley said he wanted me to take a test, in front of all the children. Naturally, they would have been disappointed if I had refused.'

'Yes, I can see that,' he nodded. 'But even so, it must have occurred to you that it was hardly what was expected of you.'

'I know, I know.' Debra compressed her lips. 'I'm sorry.'

'And is that all there was to it? This screen test?'

Debra's colour deepened. Somehow she didn't want to have to tell him about everything else, not yet. It might not be true, and it was nothing to do with him, however friendly his interest might be.

'Well, I suppose so,' she temporised.

David Hollister studied her confused expression. 'Dominic McGill—whom we have all heard of; a man with numerous plays and films to his credit; who lives an entirely different life from any you have known, or

34

me, for that matter; this man takes the trouble to find out your name and telephone number from the school principal, just because you've taken a screeen test that has apparently been successful! My dear Debra, the mind boggles!'

Debra stared miserably at her fingernails. 'Please, Mr. Hollister—David, then,' as he protested, 'don't ask me any more now. There is more, I admit it, but just at this moment I don't want to say any more.'

Hollister looked a little annoyed, but he shrugged his shoulders and ran a hand over his thinning brown hair. 'I can't make you, of course.' he said slowly. 'But if I were you, I would think carefully before getting involved with a man like McGill. At the moment, he's only a voice over the telephone; when you meet him you may be able to understand what I mean.'

'Oh, but ...' began Debra, starting to tell him about McGill's visit to her apartment, and then she stopped.

Misunderstanding her, Hollister continued: 'I know you're going to say you can take care of yourself, but really, Debra, the film world is a very big jungle, swarming with wild animals. It's kill or be killed, and quite frankly, I don't think you have the proportions of a lady-killer.'

Debra smiled at his humour, but said nothing.

Hollister offered her a cigarette, and when they were both smoking, he said: 'I'd like to think you'd think of me as someone you could turn to, if you found yourself out of your depth.'

'Thank you.' Debra felt grateful to him.

'Well, as I've said, be careful. Remember what I've told you. No matter how much they flatter you, don't be misled.'

'I ... I won't,' murmured Debra, wishing now he would let it go. But instead he returned to the subject of Dominic McGill.

35

'Tell me,' he said, 'do you know much about McGill?'

'Practically nothing,' replied Debra truthfully.

'Then remember, as a jungle animal, there is no one more dangerous.'

Debra drew on her cigarette to avoid a reply, and he looked at her a little irritatedly.

'I do know what I'm talking about,' he said. 'He's completely without scruples, either morally or financially. The press can't leave him alone. He's *news!*' He said the word with vehement dislike, and Debra wondered fleetingly whether in actual fact David Hollister didn't envy, just a little, the life that Dominic McGill apparently led.

She looked at Hollister uncertainly. 'If you think he's particularly interested in me, you couldn't be more wrong,' she said. 'It ... it's not exactly a personal thing.'

This of course intrigued David Hollister even more, and she could tell he was becoming more curious than ever. So changing the subject, she began talking about the sports they had in England, most particularly British football which was becoming more popular in the United States. David Hollister had no choice but to follow her lead, for without labouring the point there was nothing more he could say.

That evening Debra went to the movies with Margaret Stevens, the teacher who took classes in music and drama. Margaret was a girl in her late twenties, unmarried now, although she had been married and divorced several years before. She was a cynic so far as men were concerned, and Debra didn't take her comments about the opposite sex too seriously.

She had not, of course, heard about Debra's screen test, and for a few hours Debra determinedly put all thoughts of it out of her mind. The film, a powerful police thriller, was sufficient to occupy her thoughts, although she stiffened when she read in the credits that the screen play had been written by Dominic McGill. Was she to have no peace now? she thought angrily. Until then she had never bothered to read the credits.

Afterwards they called in a coffee bar and had hamburgers and coffee, and discussed the film. When Debra returned to the apartment she felt pleasantly tired, and thought she would sleep without much difficulty. But once she was alone in bed, her thoughts turned back tortuously to the problem at the front of her mind, and she lay for hours puzzling the circumstances of her birth. Eventually, when she did get to sleep, she slept soundly and dreamlessly, not waking until after ten o'clock.

Immediately her thoughts leapt to the remembrance that McGill was arriving at eleven o'clock to take her —where? She shook her head, slid out of bed, and washed hastily while the percolator bubbled appetizingly. She dressed in a slim-fitting suit of orange tweed, that suited her very well. With her dark hair and lightly tanned complexion, it was very attractive, and even the skirt, which Aunt Julia had said was too short, looked all right with her two-inch heels. She left her hair loose, and it curved confidingly round her chin. She was gulping down her third cup of coffee when the bell rang. She swallowed quickly, almost choked herself, and went to the door realising she had forgotten to put on any make-up.

Dominic McGill was waiting outside, looking tall and relaxed in a biscuit-coloured suit, a cream shirt, and a brown knitted tie. His hair, which he wore cut very short on top, was a little unruly from the hectic breeze outside, and lay half over his forehead. He brushed it back with a careless hand and said:

37

'Hi. You're ready after all. I had an idea you'd cry off at the last minute.'

Debra looked at him momentarily, liking what she saw, and then she said: 'Just a minute. I want to put on some lipstick.'

He raised his shoulders indolently, swinging his car keys. 'Okay. Make it quick!'

For a moment she resented his tone, then hastily grabbed her make-up bag and extracted the pink lipstick and quickly applied it to her mouth, looking in the mirror to make sure it was not smudged. Then she lifted her black patent handbag, and said: 'I'm ready!'

He stood back so that she could precede him down the stairs, and she went down awkwardly, overwhelmingly conscious of him behind her. Outside, parked in a 'No waiting' area, was a dark green car of generous proportions, twin exhausts heralding the power that Debra was sure was beneath the bonnet. McGill swung open the passenger door, and Debra took a deep breath, then slid in, tucking her skirt round her legs, a little self-conscious of the shortness of the skirt now. But Dominic McGill didn't even look at her knees as he slid in, inserting the keys casually in the ignition. When he turned on the engine, there was a powerful roar, and Debra tensed a little. If she had been nervous in the buses, what would she be like in this thing!

Surprisingly, though, she could relax with him. He drove fast but expertly, and even the terrifying descent from the heights to the harbour didn't frighten her. She looked at his lean, tanned hands on the wheel. They were long-fingered, hard hands, which she felt sure could be powerful, too, if their owner desired it. There was nothing gentle about him, and she wondered on what particular stories David Hollister had based his opinion of him. As she spent more time with him she could see that to some women he would be irresistible. Women who liked men to be brutal, and treat them like chattels.

Surprised at her thoughts, she half-smiled to herself, and he glanced at her as she did so, and said: 'What's so funny?'

Debra shook her head. 'Nothing really.' She flushed. 'What—what sort of car is this?'

He negotiated a sharp bend and turned the car on to the main highway out of the city, before replying. 'A Ferrari,' he remarked casually. 'Have you heard of it?'

'Of course.' Debra swallowed hard. A Ferrari, no less! No matter what happened now, she would certainly have something to remember when all this was over. 'Does—does it do over a hundred?'

He smiled sardonically. 'Just about,' he remarked, and then relented. 'Sure, it goes much faster than that. Do you want me to show you?'

'Oh, no! That is—no, thank you.' Debra looked out of the window. She was interested in where they were going, and wished he would tell her now, instead of leaving her wondering. She had never been far out of the city, and this was an entirely new direction for her. They were driving along the highway that ran beside the ocean, and it was startlingly beautiful. The breakers creamed on to the shoreline below them, while the blue of the sky seemed to melt into the horizon. Dominic McGill had the front windows of the car open, and the fresh breeze cooled the atmosphere in the vehicle. Debra rested her arm on the open window ledge and felt a sense of wellbeing pervade her whole body. It was such a glorious day, and even her eventual facing of this problem that troubled her could not douse her enjoyment of the day.

About an hour from San Francisco, he turned off the main highway on to a lesser road that wound up into the hills. A private road curving to the left was tree-lined and shady, and it was on to this that Dominic turned the powerful automobile. Debra glanced at him.

'Where are we going?' she asked at last, unable to prevent her curiosity.

He glanced at her. 'I thought you were the girl who didn't want to know,' he said lazily. 'Don't tell me I've aroused your interest at last!'

Debra half-smiled. 'Actually, you have. Where are you taking me?'

'Wait a few minutes longer, and you'll find out,' he said, grinning, and she was caught again by the boyish quality of his smile. She looked away from him. This was no good, she was behaving foolishly, allowing him to get under her guard like this. Heavens, she had hardly known him five minutes; she must control her enjoyment of trips like this. She was as susceptible to charm as the silliest teenager.

The road wound between cyprus trees, through wrought iron gates, hanging wide, and up a drive overgrown with weeds and flowering shrubs. It had once been beautiful, and there were still evidences of the landscaped gardens, and an empty swimming pool, moss-covered, was surrounded by the most expensive mosaic tiling.

Then the house came into view; an old hacienda-type dwelling, with a fountain standing idly in the courtyard before the front verandah. Dominic stopped the car, slid out, and before Debra could get out he had opened her door and helped her to her feet. She looked at Dominic and said:

'Please, tell me now. Where are we?'

Dominic McGill mounted the verandah, and pulling open the mesh door he pushed open the inner door into a wide hallway. Then he beckoned to Debra to follow him, smiling rather sardonically now.

'Welcome to the Hacienda Elizabetta!' he said mockingly.

Debra looked a little puzzled. 'The Hacienda Elizabetta?'

'Yes. This used to be Elizabeth Steel's private hide-away!'

Debra shivered a little in spite of the heat of the day. Then she walked reluctantly up the steps and across the verandah. Hesitating only momentarily, she passed Dominic McGill and walked into the dimly lit hallway. All the windows were still shuttered, but Mc-Gill walked round, opening them, letting in the brilliant sunshine to flood away all the shadows of the past.

'I ... I always thought film stars lived in Holly-wood—you know, Beverly Hills, and all that.'

Dominic McGill shrugged. 'So they do. Even Elizabeth had a house on Wilshire Boulevard. But this was where she came when she wanted complete privacy. Very few people knew this address. Come through here, and I'll show you why she liked it.'

He pushed open the double doors of a long lounge; a ghostly place, shrouded with white-sheeted furniture, and thickly covered with dust. Cobwebs hung every-where, and Debra brushed them aside, grimacing. She had never liked spiders. McGill flung open the shutters of wide french doors that opened on to the veran-dah at its western elevation. Then Debra saw the view; the height of the hacienda was deceptive, for from here they had a magnificent view of the Pacific Ocean, stretched out below them like blue silk edged with white lace. Crumbling bamboo chairs on the verandah here were positive proof that at some time someone had sat here, looking at the view in all its glory. Debra had no doubt that in the evening, with the sun setting into the ocean, it would be even more beautiful than it was at present. It was a strange and eerie thought; that the woman who had rested on this verandah might well have been her mother.

Dominic McGill seemed lost in thought, too, staring out at the view himself, as though recalling a time when things had been different. It crossed her mind momentarily to wonder how well he had known Elizabeth Steel. Of course, she would have been much older than he was, fifteen years at least, so she presumed that they had been merely acquaintances in the same business. At least, it appeared, he had been one of the very few people who had known this address.

He looked at her now, seeing the tautness of her features. 'Does it bother you?' he asked softly. 'Coming here, I mean.'

Debra looked at him. 'Should it? After all, if she was my mother, which I doubt, she never cared about me, so why should I care about her?'

'Why do you doubt it so much? The more I see of you, the more convinced I am that Morley was right. You are like her, *incredibly* like her.'

'How do you know what I'm like?'

He looked bored. 'Come on, come on! I don't know what you're like—as a person. You naturally have your own personality. There are other things, less tangible things, that connect, somehow. The way you look when you're angry, the way you twist your fingers together, the way you walk, and move your head. It's no good, Debra. You have too much going for you.'

Debra compressed her lips, annoyed that he had called her by her Christian name, without her consent. She walked back into the hall, and looked up the flight of stairs to the floor above.

Without her being aware of it, he came behind her, and she jumped when he said: 'Do you want to see your mother's room?'

Debra glared at him. 'She might *not* have been my mother! And no, I've seen enough. Why did you bring me here, anyway? It's a horribly gloomy place.'

'It didn't used to be,' he remarked, closing the shutters again in the long lounge. Then he closed the hall shutters, and Debra thankfully pushed open the mesh door, and emerged into the sunshine. 'When Elizabeth was alive, it was never gloomy.'

'Why hasn't it been sold?' asked Debra, kicking a stone.

Dominic locked the doors. 'Who would sell it? She had no heirs. Everything has been left as it was, mainly I guess because Aaron is such a sentimentalist.'

Debra leaned against the bonnet of the powerful car, but straightened when Dominic McGill remarked that it was dusty after the journey. Brushing down her skirt, she accepted a cigarette from him with ill grace. Then she said, through a cloud of smoke:

'Tell me something: if Elizabeth Steel was my mother, who was my father? Am I illegitimate?'

McGill blew a smoke ring lazily, and then smiled. 'Illegitimate? What a terrible word! Would it matter to you if you were?'

Debra swallowed hard. 'Yes.'

'Why? You weren't responsible.'

'I know—but there's a stigma attached, all the same.'

'Imagination,' he remarked, looking amused still.

'You know nothing about it,' she stormed at him angrily. 'You seem to think you can tell me anything, and I should just be able to accept it—like that!' She rubbed her nose thoughtfully. 'I always thought my parents died in a train crash. I wish they had.'

'Oh, grow up!' He looked disgusted now.

43

'Well!' Debra drew on her cigarette. 'Anyway, surely you must have some idea—if this woman had a baby, people would *know*!'

'And that's the only point against this claim,' he said, nodding. 'So far as Emmet can remember, Elizabeth worked solidly until about 1965 when we know she took six months' holiday, on doctor's orders. She went to Fiji, in the Philippines.' He smiled slowly and reminiscently, and Debra looked at him strangely.

'How old are you, Mr. McGill?' she asked, frowning.

'Thirty-nine. Why?'

'Just curiosity,' she replied, walking across the gravel sweep to the side of the house where that wonderful view was visible. He followed her, the soles of his suede shoes crunching on the stones. She looked up at him for a moment, meeting his eyes. They were so *blue*, she thought inconsequently, and then colouring, she looked away feeling gauche. 'So you would be twenty-three, in 1965,' she said, half to herself, and he nodded. 'Had . . . had you started in the business then?'

He shrugged. 'Only just,' he replied briefly. He glanced at the gold watch circling his tanned wrist. 'Come: let's go. We'll drive to San José for lunch. We pass through the Santa Clara valley on our way. The fruit groves are blooming at this time of year. It's quite a sight.'

Debra walked back to the car and slid in easily. It was strange, she thought, how quickly the mind adapted itself to circumstances. She would never have believed a week ago that so many eventful things could happen to *her*. And to imagine what Aunt Julia would think of her exploring the countryside in company with *Dominic McGill* was laughable, really. She would be scandalised!

44

When he climbed in beside her, she looked at him. 'You didn't tell me why you brought me here.'

McGill switched on the engine before replying. 'I guess I wanted to see you here. And after all, this is only a small part of what you would inherit if you really are Elizabeth Steel's daughter. There's still the house on Wilshire Boulevard, although that is in excellent repair. Her staff of servants are still employed there. Aaron pays their salaries. It was never closed up. Her death was so unexpected.'

'I don't know what to say,' exclaimed Debra, feeling in her handbag for her cigarettes.

'What do you want?' he asked, noticing her fumbling.

'A cigarette.'

He drew out the slim gold cigarette case from his pocket, flicked it open, and she took one of the long American cigarettes from it. Then he tossed his lighter into her lap, and she lit the cigarette gratefully. 'Thank you.'

He nodded and put the lighter back in his pocket. 'Now, tell me about your life in England.'

Debra sighed. 'There's very little to tell. My life has been singularly uneventful, *so far!*' and she smiled when she saw his humorous expression. 'It's true. I teach at the Valleydown Secondary School, and I live with Aunt Julia. When you've said that, you've said it all.'

He shook his head. 'And you are *content*?'

'I suppose I am. I like reading, you see, and classical music, and it doesn't take much to entertain me.'

He gave a short laugh. 'God, what a life!'

Debra smoked her cigarette in silence, content to gaze out of the window. The journey to San José was accomplished swiftly. Once on to Route 101, Dominic McGill opened up the powerful engine, and the Fer-

45

rari responded effortlessly. Debra glanced once at the speedometer and read its dial disbelievingly. Then she glanced at her companion, seeing the intense concentration on his face, and decided to say nothing. It was obvious he had complete control of the automobile, and the outside world had temporarily ceased to exist for him.

They ate at a motel restaurant on the outskirts of the city. It was an enormous place, cabanas set around a swimming pool providing the individual accommodation. The restaurant had a glass floor through which a gigantic aquarium was visible below them. Debra gazed about her in astonishment, following Dominic McGill and a white-coated attendant across to a table in one corner. Potted plants in huge bases clung tenaciously over the trellises which divided the tables, while a four-piece group of Mexican entertainers played unobtrusively on a small dais near the bar. Their table was set by a wide glass-paned wall that overlooked the swimming pool, and the highway beyond.

Dominic McGill ordered Martinis, his own laced with gin, and then they studied the enormous menus, Debra unable to decide from so many exciting dishes which to choose. McGill looked at her over the top of his menu and grinned lazily. 'Well?' he said. 'Have you decided?'

Debra shook her head, liking the crinkly, humorous lines around his eyes. 'Would you—I mean—you decide?'

He studied her momentarily, and then returned to the menu. 'Okay, we'll have avocado cocktail, steaks, and lemon soufflé, does that sound all right?'

Debra put her menu aside. 'It sounds wonderful!' She accepted another cigarette, and after it was lit, she said: 'This is a marvellous place, isn't it?'

'It's okay.' He looked sardonic. 'You're easily satisfied.'

Debra flushed, and he bit his lip. 'I'm sorry,' he said shortly. 'I guess that was unkind.'

Debra did not reply, but her cheeks continued to burn. He must think her an awfully old-fashioned creature. Probably the women he was used to associating with could verbally spar with him much more successfully than she could. All she seemed to do was act like a teenager who had never been taken out for a meal before.

Dominic McGill studied her expression. She had a very revealing countenance, although she was unaware of it. She was also unaware of the attractive picture she made in her orange suit, her sleek swathe of dark hair falling like a curtain of silk across her cheeks.

The meal was delicious, but Debra purposely refrained from enthusing over it. Instead, she concentrated on enjoying it, and the red wine which he had ordered to go with the food. Unused to alcohol, she was vaguely aware that she was drinking rather too much, but she did not want to appear gauche, so she drank her Martini, and three glasses of wine, and even had several sips of the brandy which accompanied their coffee.

Her head swam a little as she smoked her final cigarette, but she determinedly shook the feeling off, and tried to interest herself in the rhythmic music coming from the quartet. They had not spoken much during the meal, but now he looked at her intently, and said:

'Did you like it?'

Debra fingered the collar of her suit, widening her eyes to get things into focus. 'Very much,' she said, nodding, and then finding the up-and-down motion of her head made her feel rather sick, she stopped.

47

'Good.' He glanced at his watch. 'It's half after three. Shall we go?'

Debra glanced round. The distance between their table and the door seemed a terribly long way, and she felt nervously apprehensive of standing up. What if she couldn't make it to the door? Her legs felt awfully weak, and her head felt nauseously light. It would be terrible if she made a fool of herself, and embarrassed him *here*.

With trembling hands she pushed back her chair and stood up. The room swam around her, and she gripped the table tightly, like a non-swimmer hanging on to the rail at the swimming pool. She was unaware of Dominic McGill moving, until she felt his hand grip her upper arm in a vice-like hold and he said:

'Come on, kid. Don't pass out on me here.'

Debra pushed back her hair, looking up at him. 'I ... I'm all right,' she said tightly, resenting his tone.

'Oh, yeah! Can you make the door, do you suppose?'

Debra squared her shoulders. 'Of course.'

He shook his head, and without giving her time to protest he propelled her firmly to the swing doors of the restaurant. Outside, when the heat of the afternoon sun hit her, she almost staggered under its onslaught, but with intense self-control she managed to walk with him across to the car.

Once there, she leaned against the bonnet, uncaring of the dust on her skirt now, and tried to clear her muzzy brain. McGill watched her for a few minutes, then walking round the car, he opened his door, and slid in. Debra watched him detachedly, as a spectator watches something going on of which he has no active part. She felt terrible, and what was more, it infuriated her. She ought to be able to have a couple of drinks without feeling like this, she thought, angrily.

Heavens, she had known of alcohol long before her trip to San Francisco. Was she always to appear in this completely ridiculous light whenever he was around?

He had got out of the car again now, and was coming back round to her. He opened his hand and she saw two small pills lying on his palm. 'Take them,' he said, nodding. 'You'll feel better when you have.'

Debra hesitated. 'I—I'll feel better directly,' she protested.

'Not for some time,' he remarked, looking at her intently. 'You're what we would loosely call *slung*,' he half-smiled. 'Now, be a good girl, and take them.'

Debra compressed her lips, but she took the tablets, and swallowed them without difficulty. Then he opened the car door, and she collapsed inside. He got in beside her, his arm along the back of the seat. 'Interesting,' he said mockingly. 'What you've been giving me has been the truth.'

'What do you mean?' she asked tiredly, running a hand round the back of her neck, under her hair.

'The kind of life you used to lead; I guess I thought you might conceivably be exaggerating.' He frowned. 'It puzzles me why your aunt, if that's who she is, should keep a thing like this from you. She must be one hell of a bitter person.'

'Why?'

He shrugged. 'It stands to reason that she would only deprive you of what is rightfully your choice if she was jealous. If she was Elizabeth's sister, she had plenty to be jealous about.'

'How well did you know Elizabeth Steel?' Debra was beginning to feel a little better.

He swung round to the wheel. 'Well enough,' he said shortly. 'Shall we go?'

He dropped her at her apartment in San Francisco as the evening shadows were beginning to lengthen.

Debra wanted to ask what would happen now, but he had been silent on the journey from San José, and she had the feeling that he had resented her questioning him about Elizabeth Steel. So she watched the powerful green car zoom away down the hill, then walked wearily into the apartment block. The throbbing beat of the guitars from the apartment above hers were only a background to the throbbing of her head, and she felt depressed and miserable, like she had never been before.

CHAPTER FOUR

FOR almost a week Debra heard no more, and she was half beginning to believe that she had imagined the whole affair. It all had a dreamlike quality anyway, and only her remembrance of Dominic McGill disturbed her emotional balance.

Then, on the Friday morning when she had a free period at Filbert, David Hollister sent for her. Putting away her books, she wondered what on earth he could have to say to her. She hoped he was not going to start talking about the screen test again, and reviving all the worries that she had managed to put to the back her mind.

But when she arrived at David Hollister's door, he admitted her into his study with a very thoughtful expression marring his good looks. A tall broad man stood near the wide windows which overlooked the playing fields, and it was to him that Debra's eyes were drawn. He was very dark-skinned, and his hair was greying now but it had once been black. He was handsome in a strong aquiline way, and she thought he must be in his sixties. He stared disconcertingly at Debra, and shook his head disbelievingly.

'Dom was right,' he muttered, almost to himself. 'Good God! It's uncanny!'

David Hollister looked at Debra reprovingly. 'This is Mr. Aaron Johannson, Debra,' he said. 'He tells me that he believes you are Elizabeth Steel's daughter.'

Debra sighed. 'Does he? Oh, well, I suppose he's also told you that that's why there was so much excitement when I went to the studios.'

'Yes, he has.' David Hollister looked reproachful.

'Debra, why didn't you tell me, when I asked you? Surely you could have confided in *me*!'

'Oh, David——' she began, but Aaron Johannson came forward and took her hand, ignoring the other man completely.

'Debra, my dear,' he said, shaking his head. 'Have you any idea what a feeling of satisfaction it gives me to see you? Elizabeth was—well, there was no one quite like her, and seeing you now—when I believed on Elizabeth's death that I should never see her likeness again—excites me beyond expression. There are so many things we have to say to one another. So much to do!'

Debra moved restlessly. 'Mr. Johannson, surely you realise that all this is just speculation? I mean, Mr. McGill must have told you the facts. I know nothing, nothing whatsoever, about Elizabeth Steel. I was brought up by my aunt to believe that my parents died in a train crash when I was a baby. This may yet be so. People have doubles, you know.'

Aaron Johannson shook his head. 'My dear, there is so much more than mere likeness between you. Dominic has told me everything, as you say, but he has reinforced it with his opinion that you are like her in many other ways. And he knew Elizabeth so well—I'm prepared to accept his decision until it's proved wrong.'

Debra heaved a sigh. 'Honestly, it's all crazy to me! I can't possibly be this woman's daughter. I just can't. Besides, even if I am, what does it matter?'

Aaron Johannson raised a hand protestingly. 'Debra, Debra, calm down! Of course there's much more to be said and done. Look, I want you to come with me now. I have a luncheon today, at the Royal Bay Hotel. I want you to come with me. I can't miss this engagement, but we can talk while we eat. I *must* know more about you. Mr. Hollister, you will let her go, will you not?'

'Oh, but——' began Debra, only to be silenced by David Hollister, as he said:

'Of course. It may be that Miss Warren will not wish to return to her teaching position here. If this is so, I shall have to inform the governors...'

'Mr. Hollister!' exclaimed Debra. 'Please don't do that. Give me a little time. I'm sure this is all *mad*!'

Hollister frowned. 'And this afternoon? Will you be back to take your usual classes?'

'Yes——'

'No.' It was Aaron Johannson. 'No, she will not be back today. Keep her position open if you will, but if Miss Warren is Elizabeth Steel's daughter, there's much to be done.'

Debra looked exasperatedly at Johannson. 'This is my life you're disarranging.'

'I know. And you'll thank me for doing so.' Not waiting to listen to any protestations, he hustled her to the door. 'You will excuse us, Mr. Hollister, but we're late.'

Debra looked back at David Hollister pleadingly. 'I'm sorry, David,' she said, 'but what can I do?'

Hollister shrugged. 'Nothing, I guess. Okay, Debra. We'll see you Monday morning.'

Aaron Johannson had a chauffeur-driven Jenson outside, and Debra only had time to collect her coat before she was helped into the back of the car, and Aaron Johannson slid in beside her. He leaned forward, gave the chauffeur her address, and then leaning back, said:

'You'll change, of course.'

Debra looked annoyed. 'Do I have any choice? Really, Mr. Johannson, I don't like this high-handed treatment. I'm a human being, not a machine, you know.'

The film producer looked at her steadily. 'Now, I'll tell you something,' he said. 'You were born in 1959, right?'

Debra nodded.

'I happen to know that in 1959 Elizabeth suffered a nervous breakdown, or that's the story. It was hushed up, of course, and she flew to England, to a clinic there, to recuperate. With a couple of films in the can, we were able to spread them over the period she was away, just enough to disguise her absence from the press.'

Debra swallowed hard. 'Oh, God!'

'Yes, and that's not all.'

'What more could there be?' Debra was attentive now, her eyes wide.

Johannson now took a deep breath, and for a moment he looked very old. 'Something that was not generally known,' he said heavily. 'And I'm only telling you now because I think you ought to know. Elizabeth and I were married in 1956.'

'What!' Debra pressed the palms of her hands to her cheeks. 'Oh!' She shook her head weakly. 'Does—does Dominic McGill know this?'

'That I was Steel's husband? No. She never wanted to advertise it after its usage had grown stale.'

Debra stared at him. 'What does that mean?'

He shrugged, giving a short mirthless laugh. 'It means, my dear, that Elizabeth Steel married me because by doing so she achieved what she had wanted all along—fame and fortune, and the chance to use her great talent in films worthy of its calibre.'

'Oh, Mr. Johannson!' Debra was shocked.

He half-smiled. 'Don't feel sorry for me. I knew what I was doing. And when other, younger men came along, I just turned a blind eye to her infidelities. Her talent was such that to produce a film she was in was a thrill beyond compare. She was a dream to watch. And I adored her.' Then he looked at Debra steadily. 'If you are Elizabeth's daughter, then you are my daughter too, and for this I can never forgive her. That she should choose to keep so important a thing to herself....' His voice trailed away. 'I can see why, of course. Children, no matter how delightful, can be terribly ageing, for no matter how old we look our children are mute witnesses to our maturity. So it was with Elizabeth—her beauty, her youth, meant everything to her.' He shook his head. 'We must find out the truth, of course, but I'm convinced now that you are my daughter, *Elizabeth's* daughter.'

Debra felt like crying. The week of uncertainty, combined with this revelation of her parentage, were disturbing knives of emotional torture. She felt an intense feeling of compassion for this man, who had so loved Elizabeth Steel, that he had wanted her to stay with him, whatever the humiliation he had to bear.

Johannson looked at her compassionately. 'So you see,' he said, 'I think I have the right to dictate a little in this affair. I want to know the truth as much as you do.' He smiled. 'And now we're here at your apartment. Are you going to invite me in?'

Debra smiled back at him, and nodded. 'Of course, Mr. Johannson,' she said.

'You'd better make it Aaron,' he remarked, as they mounted the stairs to the apartment. 'You can hardly make it anything else, but Mr. Johannson is so cold— so formal.'

'All right—Aaron.' She smiled again, and inserted her key in the lock.

During the rest of that eventful day, Debra got to know the famous producer very well indeed. They seemed to be able to talk together so easily, and in a short period she realised she had practically related her whole life story. In return, he told her a lot about himself, and his work, and about the enigma that was Elizabeth Steel. He spoke often, too, of Dominic McGill, making Debra overwhelmingly aware of his liking for the younger man. She herself found it difficult to speak of McGill; she was still terribly conscious of the stupid mess she had made of the lunch they had had together. What must he have thought of her? She was relieved to realise that at least he had not found it necessary to relate every detail of this to Aaron Johannson.

When the lunch was over, Aaron took her to his apartment, a penthouse high on Telegraph Hill with a marvellous view of the long waterfront which Debra liked so much. The whole block of apartments was so different from anything she had ever seen before. All the doors slid on oiled wheels, operated by a press-button mechanism, and it was luxurious beyond belief. Couches, several thicknesses of cushions deep, were upholstered in real leopard skin, while scarlet-leather armchairs invited relaxation. The carpets were in a variety of colours, from crimson to palest cream, and it was spacious enough for half a dozen people. Aaron had a couple of servants, together with his chauffeur, and he explained that they were accommodated in a separate block, adjacent to this one. Only his manservant, a giant called Barnabas, lived in, and Aaron explained that he could do anything, from cooking and cleaning, to washing, and acting as valet when necessary.

Debra, despite her nervousness, found it easy to make herself at home. Whether it was the tenuous thread of a possible relationship between this man and herself she wasn't sure, but she did know that she liked him immensely, and could relax in his company. He put on the stereo for her while he went to arrange for some coffee, and she slipped off her shoes and curled up on the couch. She had had a cocktail, and a brandy at lunchtime, and she felt pleasantly comfortable. She lit a cigarette, and when Aaron returned he smiled.

'You look right, somehow,' he said, his eyes gentle. 'Oh, Debra, you've no idea how much I hope you are *my* daughter, Elizabeth's daughter!'

Debra looked compassionately at him. 'Why?'

He sighed. 'I loved Elizabeth, more than anything else in the world. There was no one like her. No one to ever take her place—but now....' He shook his head. 'If you are her daughter—things will change, it will be *wonderful*!'

Debra studied the tip of her cigarette. 'And if I am—Elizabeth's daughter, what do you expect me to do?'

Aaron looked puzzled. 'I don't understand you. What do you mean?'

Debra looked disturbed. 'Aaron, you seem to be forgetting Aunt Julia. She's the only relation I've ever known. And then there's this,' she waved her hand around the sumptuous apartment. 'I think it's wonderful, *fantastic*, but it's not my world, not the world I've been used to. I *like* teaching. I suppose that sounds strange to you, but I do!'

Aaron seated himself opposite her, frowning. 'Debra, if you are my daughter, naturally I shall expect you to stay here—in the States, where you belong.'

Debra shook her head, unwillingly shrugging away the picture of Dominic McGill that came to her mind. It was terrible the way that man was disturbing her emotionally. Particularly as she knew he wasn't at all interested in her except as a physical replica of an actress he had once known well.

'I couldn't do that,' she said. 'Don't you see, Aaron, you've made your life without Elizabeth. And I have to go back. I couldn't abandon Aunt Julia.'

'Your aunt could come and live here too,' exclaimed Aaron expansively. 'This place is only a temporary home for me. My house is further south, in Los Angeles. We could all live there——'

'My aunt hates America,' said Debra, shaking her head. 'She didn't want me to come. It was only realising how badly it would look to the school authorities if I refused after applying that forced her hand. She's rather possessive, I'm afraid. But I'm used to it now. I couldn't hurt her.'

'Has it ever occurred to you how much she may have hurt you?' asked Aaron, his eyes dark with concern. 'Don't you see? If you are who we think you are, then this is only half the story. Why your aunt concealed the truth from you for so long is another story altogether. Do you see that?'

Debra frowned. So far she had refused to consider this angle.

Aaron pressed home his advantage. 'Didn't Dominic query this?'

Debra flushed. 'He may have done. I don't remember.' She stubbed out her cigarette. 'Does—does Mr. McGill live in this block of apartments, too?'

'Dominic? Heavens, no! He doesn't live in 'Frisco. His home is in Santa Monica, out of Los Angeles. Didn't he tell you?'

Debra shook her head. 'But he came to my apartment, to see about the test and everything. I thought he must live in San Francisco.'

'As you get to know Dom better you will discover that he's a fanatic so far as speed is concerned. Sure the studio contacted him, Emmet Morley that is, and I guess he flew up from L.A. to see you.'

'*Flew up?*' echoed Debra.

'Sure. He owns a small jet, flies it himself.'

'I see.' Debra felt astounded. 'So last Sunday, when he took me out to see Elizabeth Steel's house near San José, he had *flown* from Los Angeles that morning?'

'I guess so. It doesn't take him long. And then he has the Ferrari. I've known him *drive* up in less than five hours.'

'Heavens!' Debra's eyes were wide.

'What did you think of Dominic, anyway?' asked Aaron. 'I guess you've heard of him.'

'Oh, yes, I've heard of his writing.' She looked down at her finger nails. 'David—David Hollister, that is, says he attracts publicity.'

Aaron laughed. 'That's putting it mildly,' he said, sobering. 'Naturally he attracts publicity. He's bound to. Women like him, and the press like picturing him with some glamorous dame. They like to print the gossip about him, and there's always plenty of that. But he's no boy after all, and he hasn't gotten to the age of thirty-nine without learning something about life.'

Debra felt her cheeks burning for no reason. 'Is he married?'

'No. He's never been married. There have been a couple of girls who he went around with longer than the rest, and there was plenty of speculation, but I guess he finds it's not necessary.' He studied Debra's expression. 'Don't look like that. You're surely not naive enough to believe that a man like Dominic could live like a celibate?'

Debra shook her head. 'It's not that. I suppose no one ever put a thing like that into words for me before.'

Aaron looked contrite. 'Debra, I'm sorry. I guess I get so used to talking to the hard-faced set around the

59

studios, I never thought! I'm sorry.'

Debra managed a tight smile, but she was disturbed more than she liked to think. But it was not a personal thing, but rather an intensive feeling of disgust at the kind of life Dominic McGill led, she thought, wrinkling her nose.

There was the sound of a key being inserted in the door of the apartment, and somebody let themselves into the hall, and then entered the huge lounge where Aaron and Debra were sitting.

Aaron got to his feet, grinning wryly, and Debra glanced round interestedly, only to turn swiftly round again, her heart thumping.

'Hi, Dom,' said Aaron, half-amusedly. 'Talk of the devil!'

Dominic McGill walked lazily round the couch so that he could see Debra's embarrassed face. He smiled mockingly, and said:

'And what have you been saying about me, Miss Warren?'

'Oh, call her Debra,' said Aaron, before Debra could answer. 'We've merely been discussing the question of your publicity!'

'Bad, most of it,' he said, grinning. 'Why? Where do I figure in all this?'

Debra refused to meet his eyes. In the brief moment she had looked at him she had registered everything about him, from the light blue suit he was wearing to the rolled-neck white shirt that suited him so well. His clothes were always immaculate, and his lean body looked very well in them.

Aaron shrugged. 'You know perfectly well, Dom, that wherever you go there's someone ready to do your advertising for you. In this case, David Hollister seems to have been bugging you.'

Debra's eyes widened. 'I didn't say that.'

'In time you'll realise that people like Hollister adore scandal.' Aaron grimaced. 'I guess that's a fair comment on your life, isn't it, Dom?'

McGill looked at the older man amiably. 'I guess so. Now—what gives? When you rang earlier I was very busy.'

Aaron laughed. 'Were you? Well, I won't ask at what! I—I haven't gotten around to discussing it with Debra yet.'

'Discussing what?' Now Debra looked up, her eyes going from Aaron to Dominic McGill, and then back again to Aaron. 'What is this?'

McGill helped himself to a drink, a tall glass of some green liquid that he swallowed like beer. Noticing her curious eyes, he said, nodding to his drink: 'Lime and lemon. That's all!' No alcohol!'

Debra looked away. He seemed determined to embarrass her still more.

Aaron seated himself beside Debra, taking one of her hands in his.

'Debra darling,' he murmured, 'I've given this matter some thought since I got Dom's call in Madrid.'

'A call—to *Madrid*?'

'Sure. How else did I know you were here?'

'But I thought—I mean—Mr. McGill said you were filming and would probably see me when you got back.'

'So I was. But Dom also knew that I wasn't expected back for another couple of months, and that you might have returned to England by then. So he rang me. Believe me, I was delighted!'

Debra shook her head. Opulent apartments, fast cars, film stars and calls to Madrid were commonplace things to them.

Aaron went on: 'So, as I said, after receiving Dom's call, I realised that the only way to get to the bottom of this was to go to England and see your so-called Aunt Julia!'

'Go to England?' echoed Debra.

'Yes, England. Debra, don't *you* want to know the truth?'

'Well, yes, I suppose so. But I mean, I'm working here. I don't expect to go home for another three months.'

Aaron shook his head. 'Look, honey, this isn't going to cost you a cent. This is my trip. Call it a present, if you like. At least it's a way of seeing you—seeing a lot of you, for a couple of weeks. Honey, after all I've told you....' He bent his head. 'Can you refuse me?'

Debra felt tangled up inside, and when she looked up into Dominic McGill's sardonic face she felt suddenly breathless.

'Oh, Aaron,' she began helplessly, and he looked expectantly at her. 'I—I just can't leave the school without losing my job! And I don't want to lose my job. I like it here, I like my freedom....'

'Didn't you have any freedom in England?' asked McGill, studying her intently.

Debra moved awkwardly under his scrutiny. 'My—my aunt is rather strict. Besides, we weren't terribly well off....'

Aaron squeezed her hand. 'Debra honey, there's no reason why you can't come back to the States. Okay, so you lose your job. I'll find you another one, if that's what you want. You can stay as long as you like. If you are....' he hesitated, only momentarily, 'Elizabeth's daughter, then this could be your home.'

Debra shook her head. 'Aaron, you're sweet, and I think you're a marvellous man, but I couldn't just ... just allow you to support me, even temporarily.'

'Why not?' It was Dominic who spoke.

Debra continued to look at Aaron. 'Because I

honestly don't believe I am Elizabeth Steel's daughter
... or anything! I'm just plain ordinary Debra Warren,
from Valleydown in Sussex.'

'No one could call you plain or ordinary,' muttered
Aaron violently. 'Debra, this means everything to me.
Please, whatever you decide to do afterwards, and I
promise I'll abide by your decision, please let me
satisfy myself that you are ... Elizabeth's daughter!'

Debra bent her head. It was terribly hard to refuse
him. After all, she thought wildly, this man might be
her father! Could she deny her own father, a man who
scarcely had had a wife, let alone a daughter, the right
to discover the truth? Basically she knew that the
thought of facing the truth frightened her. If she was
who he thought she was then it created so many more
problems.

'I don't know....' she began helplessly. 'There's still
my job....'

McGill shrugged. 'Easily fixed!' he remarked. 'It's
your decision.'

Debra twisted her hands together. 'Aaron, please, I
need time.' She sighed. 'This has all happened too
quickly, too suddenly. It's unbelievable.'

'All right, I'll give you time,' he said, standing up
wearily. 'But only until Monday. That gives you two
clear days to think about it.'

During the next two days Debra was given ample
opportunity for thought. She realised that Aaron was
being completely fair towards her, in that he was not
using his wealth and position to influence her decision.
She spent Saturday at the Zoological Gardens, and
later sunbathed by the huge pool that adjoined it. It was
remarkable, she thought, that although she was a girl
alone in such a big city, she had never encountered
any difficult situations with men, and they seemed to

63

respect her isolation. Sometimes she wished she was more effervescent, and capable of talking to anybody, but at others she was satisfied with only her own company.

During her three months in the city, she had visited most of its places of interest. She had seen the Golden Gate park, and walked along the famous Golden Gate Bridge; she had visited the museums and churches, and explored Chinatown in daytime. At night it was a fairyland of neon signs and strip lighting, and it exuded an atmosphere of excitement. It was possible, she conceded, that had she stayed in some other city she would have felt the same, but somehow she doubted it. San Francisco was so individual, and even the gusty winds that distorted her hair with careless abandon could not dispel the charm that it held for her. She would be sorry to go back to England, whenever that might be, and although there were things in England that she knew and loved, everything here was on such a larger scale, and in a short period it had enchanted her.

On Sunday she spent the morning in the apartment, and after lunch went riding on the cable cars. Her favourite was the one that ran to Fisherman's Wharf, and then up Nob Hill, over Russian Hill and down to Bay Street. She arrived back at the apartment at six o'clock feeling pleasantly tired and she was in the bathroom when she heard her doorbell ring. Frowning, she wrapped a huge blue bath towel around her sarong-wise, and went to the door, peeping round the corner of the door with the chain still connected. As once before, Dominic McGill was standing outside, leaning indolently against the wall. He straightened when he saw her, and grinned as her face coloured in embarrassment.

'Yes?' she said quickly, hiding her bare shoulders as

well as she could.

He flicked a finger at the door. 'Open up and I'll tell you.'

'I can't,' she said shortly. 'I'm not dressed.'

'Yeah, so I see. Well, don't let it worry you. I do know what a woman looks like, you know. And you're more adequately covered than you would be on the beach.'

Debra hesitated, knowing that he was merely baiting her. Then, with resignation, she unlocked the catch and stepped back behind the door.

'Wait until I've got into the bathroom,' she said, hurrying across the floor, but he ignored her request and walked in lazily, closing the door with his back and leaning against it. Debra hastily closed the bathroom door and shot home the bolt.

Then she quickly dried herself, put on her underclothes and wrapped herself in the mauve quilted housecoat which was all she had on hand. She could not get into her bedroom without crossing the lounge and she was determined she would not do that. Then she emerged, her cheeks hot, her dark hair in disorder about her shoulders. She was unaware of the completely natural picture she created to the eyes of a man used to every artifice a woman could use to attract the opposite sex.

'Very nice,' he murmured, his eyes appraising.

Debra tried to look dignified. 'Why have you come?' She noticed he was wearing a charcoal-grey lounge suit, which contrasted sharply with the fairness of his hair and his tanned complexion. He was obviously going on somewhere.

'I've come to take you to a party,' he remarked laconically.

'Oh, but——'

'Now, don't start protesting. It's all quite legitimate

and legal. Aaron will be there later. It was his idea that you should come.'

Debra shrugged. 'What ... what sort of party is it? I mean, what do I wear? I've got no evening dresses.'

'It's not an evening dress affair. Any old thing will do. With your looks, no one's going to notice your clothes.'

Debra felt disturbed. 'I hope it's not going to be a question of everyone coming up and saying how miraculously like Elizabeth Steel I am,' she exclaimed. 'Quite frankly, I want to be *me*, not some facsimile of a film star!'

He lit a cigarette, and thrust his hands into his trousers pockets. He looked amused. 'No, I guarantee that won't happen—at least, not too frequently.'

Debra hesitated. 'I'm sorry if Aaron—Mr. Johannson, that is—has thrust the responsibility for me upon you.'

Dominic shrugged carelessly. 'It may be that I enjoy this kind of responsibility.'

Debra bent her head. 'Don't feel you have to say that,' she said awkwardly.

His eyes were narrowed, their blueness softer than usual. 'As you get to know me, you will realise that I never say anything I don't mean,' he remarked. He looked down at her, his eyes holding hers for a few moments. Debra was conscious of the throbbing beat of her heart providing competition for the guitars from the record playing in the flat above. She had never been this close to a man before, and Dominic MacGill was a very attractive man, even though she was sure, deep in her heart, that he knew it, too. She was also aware that by standing still she was inviting something of which she was as yet completely inexperienced.

He lifted the swathe of dark hair from her cheeks,

his tanned fingers hard as they brushed her cheek, and she noticed the ring he wore on the little finger of his right hand, a thick gold band inset with a huge ruby. His hand lingered in her hair, and she felt weak all over.

'Go get ready,' he murmured huskily, 'or I might do something I'd regret later. You're too much of a temptation, do you know that?'

'A temptation?' she said unsteadily.

'Sure. You're not ready for my kind of games. They don't teach that sort of thing at Filbert.'

Debra compressed her lips a little angrily. 'I'm not one of the students, you know,' she exclaimed. 'I *teach*!'

'You've still got a lot to learn,' he said, smiling, showing his even white teeth. 'Go on, be quick!'

Debra moved away with a strange kind of reluctance, hating herself inwardly for behaving like that in the first place. He would be bound to think she was as gullible as any of the children from the school. Determinedly, straightening her shoulders, she marched into her bedroom and slammed the door. She leaned back against it, gathering herself mentally. She would never have believed she could act so foolishly.

She slid back the doors of her wardrobe. Her collection of clothes looked lost inside. She had not been able to bring a lot of things with her and she felt impatient with herself for not providing more choice. She hadn't done any sewing since her arrival in America, and consequently there were only two dresses to choose from; a midnight blue lace, crocheted and rather attractive, or a full-skirted black chiffon, which she had never had on, mainly because Aunt Julia had said it was far too old for her. It had long full sleeves, ending in a sequinned cuff, with a cuff neckline at the front which curved low at the back.

Determinedly she pulled out the black dress. Dominic McGill would see for himself that she was no teenager! She applied a small amount of make-up, and then studied her hair. Deliberately, she wound it up into a knot on top of her head, then looked at the result. In three-inch heels, the skirt of the dress ending several inches below her knees, and the up-swept hairstyle she knew she looked years older. Satis-fied, she picked up a white silk scarf and opened her bedroom door.

She literally swept into the room, and McGill, who was lounging comfortably in one of her armchairs, studied her intently before getting slowly to his feet. He was smoking a cigar, and holding it between his teeth he walked lazily round her, making a complete circle. Debra felt terrible, particularly when he said mockingly:

'Well, no one could mistake you for one of the pupils now!'

She shrugged. 'Shall we go?'

'If you like.' He opened the door with a flourish. 'After you!'

Debra preceded him down the stairs of the block and outside. A gusty wind was blowing, and it ruffled his hair, making him look more attractive than ever. She looked about for the green Ferrari, but all she could see was a cream-coloured Cadillac, a sleek saloon, with chrome flashes. Dominic studied her for a moment, a smile playing round his lips, then he opened the nearside door of the Cadillac.

'Come on,' he said. 'We're going to be late.'

Debra stared in amazement. 'Is this yours?' she asked.

'No, I stole it,' he replied, helping her inside, and walking round the bonnet to get in beside her. 'I'm having it re-sprayed in the morning.' He started the engine, and Debra compressed her lips and refused to say anything more.

They drove out of San Francisco, north towards Sacramento. It was already after eight o'clock, and quite dark. Debra relaxed, as they drove along, content to watch his hands on the wheel, and occasionally watching the speedometer. On highways, the car raced along, an indication of the speed he loved so well, but later when they turned off the main road he slowed and there was no harsh braking on corners or jolting of his passenger.

'Where is this party?' she ventured to ask, at last.

'It's at the home of a man called Martin Bellman,' replied Dominic, glancing at her briefly. 'He and his wife have a small estate outside of town. I guess you must be hungry. You haven't eaten, have you?'

'No. But I'm not awfully hungry. Are you?'

He smiled. 'No. I'm no gourmet; food is a necessary attribute to living, but I wouldn't say I'd fold up if I didn't have a meal. You'll find there are guys who consider themselves connoisseurs of both food and wine, and spend their whole lives experimenting. In consequence they have blood pressure, and suffer from overweight problems like gout, and so on. I guess I don't want to end up like that. Steaks, cooked in the outdoors, and beer; this is good enough for me. I haven't always had the money to eat in style.'

Debra frowned, concentrating a little. 'Tell me about your life,' she said tentatively. 'How did you start writing?'

He turned into drive gates, then said: 'We're almost there, and it's a long story. I'll tell you some other time.'

Debra stifled an exclamation of annoyance. It was always the same. Whenever she attempted to learn anything about him he changed the subject.

The huge house belonging to the Bellmans was floodlit, and there were quite a few cars already parked on the gravelled forecourt. Dominic helped Debra out of the car, and they mounted the steps to double white doors which stood wide to the night air. A frilly-aproned maid took Debra's scarf and showed her through to a hall cloakroom where she could do her hair and repair any ravages to her make-up.

Debra looked about her with interest. Everywhere were evidences of the money that must have been spent, and the other women in the cloakroom looked at her speculatively. They all seemed to know one another, and she felt very isolated suddenly. She was glad to emerge and find Dominic standing in the wide, red-carpeted hallway, even though he was no longer alone, but talking to another man and two women, who turned as Debra approached, and eyed her with curiosity. Debra noticed that both the women were young, and blonde, and very chic. They sparkled with diamonds, and their clothes were obviously model dresses. The man was dark-haired and handsome, and said something in an undertone to Dominic as she got near them. Debra flushed as she saw Dominic incline his head to listen to what the other man was saying, although his eyes never left her face for an instant. Then he reached out a hand and drew her forward into the group.

'Debra, I want you to meet some friends of mine. This is Elaine Gregory, Valerie Hunter and Maxwell Bernstein.'

Debra shook hands rather reluctantly, aware that she was being thoroughly appraised, and her gown valued down to the last cent. She thought she would never be able to relax with people like this. They were too suave, too sure of themselves, and of their own ability to succeed.

'How are you liking America?' asked Maxwell Bernstein. 'I understand you were—*are*—a schoolteacher.'

'That's right,' said Debra, nodding, and glancing round her with interest.

They were standing in a wide hall, soft-carpeted, with panelled white walls, and several vases of flowers set on pedestals to provide splashes of brilliant colour. To the right, an arched entrance led into a long low lounge, which he could seee was overflowing with people. Press photographers stood in a huddle near the door, and were now eyeing Dominic with unsuppressed interest. The sound of music came from the lounge, a low intimate beat that insinuated itself sensuously into the brain.

A white-coated waiter passed with a tray of glasses of champagne, and Dominic collected two and handed one to Debra. The others had got their own, and Debra sipped the bubbling liquid, wondering whether she was going to like it. She looked at Dominic, and he grinned.

'Don't look so alarmed,' he remarked softly, so that only she could hear. 'I'm not trying to get you intoxicated.'

'I'm not alarmed,' replied Debra hotly. 'I was merely wondering whether I liked it.'

'And do you?'

'I think so.'

'I'll get you a champagne cocktail later,' he said. 'They're really something!'

Debra did not reply, wondering why she felt such a feeling of exhilaration in his company. She wondered why some men who were tall and dark and handsome did not disturb the senses at all, while others who were lean-faced, silvery-haired, with hard, sometimes cruel blue eyes, could arouse such a sensuous longing inside you. No wonder David Hollister resented McGill's

71

attitude!

'Here's Marsha, Dominic,' said Valerie Hunter suddenly, her slant eyes narrowing with a kind of malicious satisfaction. 'I thought it wouldn't be long before she appeared.'

Debra looked round quickly, seeing a tall slim blonde woman approaching them purposefully. She was one of the most beautiful women Debra had ever seen. Her hair was shoulder-length, tip-tilted slightly at the ends; her eyes were blue and dark-lashed, while dark brows arched questioningly. She was dressed in a skin-fitting sheath dress of some clinging material, its blueness accentuating the blueness of her eyes. Debra looked up at Dominic who had also looked towards the newcomer, but he did not look at all perturbed, and when the blonde reached them he merely smiled sardonically, and said:

'Hi.'

'You're late, darling,' she said, sliding her arm possessively through his. 'I've been waiting for you.'

Dominic McGill did not apologise. Instead he said: 'Debra, this is Marsha Mathews. Marsha, this is Debra Warren.'

'How do you do,' said Debra, but as Marsha Mathews did not offer to shake hands she did not either.

'Hello,' said Marsha coolly. 'You're Aaron's protégée, I hear.' Then she looked at Dominic. 'Darling, come on, *do*! I've got someone I want you to meet.'

Debra felt terrible now. All her earlier feelings of well-being had been dissipated by the arrival of this Marsha Mathews. She wondered how old Marsha was. Probably about twenty-seven, she surmised accurately. She certainly seemed to consider McGill her property, and Debra wondered whether Dominic liked that kind of possessive attitude. Somehow she doubted it. He was so much of an independent person.

Dominic gently but firmly disentangled himself from Marsha's hands. She looked furiously at him, and then, as though unable to prevent herself, she said pleadingly: 'Dominic, *please*!'

Dominic shrugged his shoulders, and Debra noticed that Elaine and Valerie were enjoying this exchange very much. It was obvious that they did not like Marsha Mathews, and were relishing this almost silent by-play.

Debra herself felt cold. It must be awful, she thought, to want someone so much, and to have them treat you so carelessly. She determined never to feel like that about any man. It just was not worth it.

Dominic McGill now said: 'Excuse us, won't you,' and taking Debra's arm, ignoring her astonished expression, he drew her across the hall and into the lounge where dancing was going on. Immediately, the pressmen took this as licence to take photographs, and Debra blinked rapidly as the cameras flashed in her face.

'Relax,' said Dominic, in her ear. 'Smile, and try to look as though you're enjoying yourself.'

Debra looked up at him mutinously. 'I *was* enjoying myself,' she said, in an angry tone, 'but I do not like being *used*, by you, to shake off would-be-girl-friends!'

He merely looked amused. 'Aw, come on,' he said mockingly. 'Surely you don't imagine I needed you to shake off Marsha!'

Debra flushed. 'It certainly looked like it!' she said uncomfortably.

'Baby, you don't know me very well,' he said softly. 'Come on, let's dance. Then I'll introduce you around. There are some very influential people here tonight. A lot of would-be starlets I know would give their right arm to be here.'

Debra did not reply, merely conscious of the hard strength of the fingers of the hand that had grasped hers and was pulling her after him towards the edge of the crowd where the dance floor began. The small band were playing an up-beat rhythm that Debra had only seen danced to on the television back home. She felt petrified for a moment; however would she dance to *that*? But the beat was insidious, and she felt her body swaying almost involuntarily to the sound. Then she found if she moved her feet in time the dance itself just came to her. The other young people were doing various gyrations, all variations on the same movement, and she forgot her inhibitions and allowed herself the freedom of the pulsating sound. It was exciting and hypnotic, and she forgot to be nervous. She noticed that Dominic McGill was watching her, an amused expression on his face, while he followed her effortlessly. It was apparent that he was used to this kind of dancing, for he did it well, and without affection. With his lean body and animal attraction, he could be taken for about twenty-eight, she thought breathlessly. Certainly he was not panting, as she was, when the dance ended, with the unaccustomed exercise.

'You're out of condition,' he remarked lazily. 'What do you do for exercise?'

'I walk,' said Debra indignantly. 'And I sometimes play tennis.' She frowned. 'What do you do? Apart from driving fast cars?'

'I play golf, and I swim a lot,' he replied, smiling. 'I guess you don't swim back home in Valleydown.'

'No,' replied Debra shortly. 'There's only one swimming bath in the town, and it's invariably filled with children during the times when I might be able to go.'

Dominic took her arm, and they walked across the

74

floor to where a group of men and women were standing on the edge of the dance floor.

'Elizabeth Steel's house on Wilshire has its own pool,' he remarked, dryly. 'Most large houses out here do have, you know. I have two, an indoor and an outdoor. You must come and swim with me.'

Debra compressed her lips, unable to be truthful and tell him that she couldn't swim anyway. Instead, she said: 'Thank you. I'll bear that in mind,' in a sarcastic tone of voice which made him laugh.

Then Aaron detached himself from the group they were nearing, and came towards them, holding out his hands in delighted anticipation.

'My dear Debra!' he cried enthusiastically. 'Darling, you look wonderful, doesn't she, Dom?'

Dominic moved his shoulders slightly, and Debra flushed, but she allowed Aaron to take her hands and kiss her on both cheeks, then draw her into the group preparatory to introducing her.

She met so many unfamiliar faces, with unfamiliar names attached to them, that she lost track, and it wasn't until she was sitting with Aaron and Martin Bellman himself and his wife that she realised she had not seen Dominic McGill for some time. She was sipping a glass of some cocktail which Martin Bellman had provided her with, and over its rim she surveyed the room, unwilling to admit that she was looking for McGill.

Then she saw him. He was with a crowd of younger men and girls, leaning against the low bar in the opposite corner of the room, and Marsha Matthews was leaning against him, a drink in one hand, her silver fingernails caressing the side of his neck. Debra felt sick suddenly, and stood down her cocktail, splashing a little of it as she did so. Aaron looked at her curiously, saw her pale cheeks and said:

'Of course, honey, you haven't had any supper yet. Come on, I'll take you for something to eat. You will excuse us, won't you, Lydia, Martin?'

Debra allowed Aaron to lead her out of the lounge, and into another room adjoining it, which was not so warm or smoky or crowded, and where long tables were overloaded with food of every kind. There was smoked salmon and lobster, salads and cold hams, iced soup and kebabs, sandwiches, and cheeses, fruit and trifles, and lots of creamy American coffee. Debra did not feel hungry, indeed she felt that food would choke her, but at Aaron's instigation she managed some ham and salad, and a small trifle, and after two cups of coffee she found she did feel a little better. Maybe it was Aaron's undemanding company, she thought, looking at the man gently. He was so kind and gentle, and she felt so close to him somehow.

Aaron saw her expression and interpreted it correctly, and put an arm about her slim shoulders.

'Well, Debra,' he murmured, in her ear, 'it's almost Monday. Have you reached a decision, or am I asking too soon?'

Debra looked at him fully, liking what she saw. 'Oh, Aaron,' she whispered, 'I ... I can't refuse you the right to know the truth, no more than I can deny my own curiosity. I thought it didn't matter, I didn't *want* it to matter, but it does. I'm only human, I suppose, and I want to know the truth.'

Aaron hugged her convulsively. 'Thank God for that!' he said heavily. 'You've no idea how I've felt these last couple of days, not being able to concentrate on anything. I wanted to persuade you, and I'm sure I could have persuaded you, but I wanted you to decide for yourself. It was terribly important that you should want the truth as much as me.' He laughed. 'Wait until I tell Dominic! He'll be less than surprised. He

76

was sure you would agree.'

'Oh! Was he?' Debra felt her nerves contract again.

'Sure. He's a pretty fair judge of character. I'll be interested to see what his reaction is to your Aunt Julia.'

'*My Aunt Julia!*' echoed Debra. 'But I mean, how will he meet Aunt Julia?'

'Well, quite simply, I guess. He's coming with us!'

'To *England*?' murmured Debra faintly.

'Sure. You didn't think we'd be going alone, did you?'

'Well, I....' Debra shrugged. 'I suppose I did.'

'You see, I need someone there to bear witness to what this *aunt* of yours has to say. It may not be as simple as we believe.'

Debra shivered. 'You realise that I can't believe it, even now.'

'I know, it must be even harder for you than it is for me. But, honey, you know you can't go on living a lie, if that's what it is. You have the right to everything that is mine if you are my daughter. And I need you, Debra, *believe me*! This aunt of yours can't need you more than I do.'

Debra sighed. It was terribly difficult. She had committed herself now. She must go back and discover the truth, and then.... What then? Indeed, it would be *then* that her greatest problems would face her.

And always, in the back of her mind, there was Dominic McGill. McGill, who she had imagined would fade from her thoughts once she was back in familiar surroundings, but instead he was coming with them, to England, to the places she had known all her life, and even if none of this were true, and he and Aaron returned to the States alone, she would not be able to banish his image from the recesses of her mind.

CHAPTER FIVE

DAVID HOLLISTER released Debra from her post with unconcealed misgivings. 'I think you're making a big mistake, Debra,' he said severely. 'You're throwing away everything on the chance of your being this woman's daughter. You realise, don't you, that the authorities won't allow you to return here, on this or any other teaching exchange?'

'Yes, I realise that, David,' said Debra uncomfortably. 'But it's not wholly my decision to make. If I am in reality Elizabeth Steel's daughter, then the truth should be accepted.'

David Hollister looked sardonic. 'What you mean is, the money will be very useful,' he remarked coldly. 'I didn't think you were a mercenary character, Debra. You didn't used to be.'

'Oh, honestly, I'm not!' Debra sighed. 'Can't you see that this position I am in is unacceptable now. I can't ignore the fact that Mr. Johannson loved my mother—that is—Elizabeth Steel.'

David Hollister sneered, 'You see! You're really beginning to believe it! My God, Debra, this could all be a hoax! Have you thought of that?'

'A *hoax*?' echoed Debra faintly. 'What do you mean, a hoax?'

'What I say. Sure you look like this woman, a little anyway. Maybe it's all a publicity stunt! Maybe they'll get rid of you, metaphorically speaking, once you've served whatever nefarious purpose might be behind all this.'

Debra pressed her hands to her burning cheeks. 'That's a terrible thing to say!'

'You're a naive, inexperienced child, and they're sophisticated gangsters,' muttered Hollister blackly. 'How do you know what they're really like?'

'Oh, no, David!' Debra was shaking her head. 'You're wrong! Quite wrong! I know, I just *know*, that Aaron isn't like that.'

'And McGill?'

Debra continued to shake her head. 'I don't know. But it doesn't matter. Dominic McGill has nothing to do with this.'

David Hollister snorted. 'Doesn't he? Doesn't he just? He should be able to decide whether you're Elizabeth Steel's daughter. He knew her well enough!'

Debra looked up at him with narrowed eyes. 'What do you mean?'

Hollister now looked a little embarrassed himself. 'Oh, nothing,' he muttered shortly. 'When are you leaving for England?'

Debra was glad when she left the school after that. She could sense the antagonism of the rest of the staff, engendered no doubt by David Hollister's attitude, and she felt like a deserter. Only Margaret Stevens remained her friend, and joked with her about the whole affair.

'Cinderella,' she said laughingly. 'With a wicked mother instead of two sisters.'

'Don't say that, Margaret,' exclaimed Debra, shivering. 'Like David said, it's all speculation.'

'But educated speculation,' replied Margaret thoughtfully. 'If—if Elizabeth Steel was your mother, who was your father?'

'That I don't know,' said Debra slowly. 'Maybe I'll find out if the truth comes out.'

'Have you warned your aunt of what's coming?'

'I ... no! Oh, Margaret, I couldn't suggest a thing like that in a letter, or a cable. I have to be there when

I tell her, I have to see her face to know the truth.'

'To see if she's lying,' said Margaret cynically. 'Oh, Debra, I wish this hadn't happened, for your sake. You were such a quiet, gentle girl. I don't want you to change, to become hard and brittle!' She sighed. 'But you will, you're bound to if you go on with this.'

'Why?' Debra's eyes were wide. 'Why should I?'

'Because, my love, you're associating with people and things you know nothing about, and because unless you do you'll get hurt, badly hurt. Believe me, I know. I've been through it all before.'

'You mean—men?'

'Yes, I mean men. Men like McGill, for example. Now don't tell me you haven't noticed him, because I just won't believe you.'

'Of course I've noticed him. But he's not the first man I've found attractive.'

'You admit you find him attractive?'

'Stop baiting me, Margaret,' said Debra, flushing. 'This is all so ridiculous! And I know at times I wish with all my heart I'd never arranged that trip to the Omega Studios. But I did, and Emmet Morley saw me, and now....' Her voice trailed away. 'It's become such a big thing, Margaret. It's out of my hands. I can't control it any longer. It affects other people as well as myself, and I can't take the responsibility for denying people the right to know the truth. Oh, I know I'm curious, too, I'm not denying that either, but on the other hand, the point where I could call the whole thing off has passed almost without my knowing it.'

Margaret sighed and touched Debra's arm gently. 'Well, honey, I hope you know what you're doing. I'm no maternal adviser, I know, but please take care! Don't make a fool of yourself so far as McGill is concerned.'

Debra stared at her. 'I won't,' she averred swiftly.

'I'm perfectly aware that he only sees me as a possible business proposition.'

'Maybe so. But you're a little out of his realm of comprehension, in spite of everything. And he might find it amusing to probe you.'

Debra turned away. 'Well, as I know that's all it is, how can I get hurt?' She managed a taut smile, looking back over her shoulder at her friend. 'But thanks for caring, anyway. I don't think anyone else does.'

During the days preceding their flight to England, Debra saw a lot of Aaron Johannson. He insisted on paying her fare home despite her protests, and he arranged the tickets and accommodation for the journey. He also told her they would stop over in New York for a couple of days, to allow Dominic to attend to some business he had there, and therefore give Debra a chance to see something of the city.

Debra was thrilled. On her journey out to San Francisco they had only spent a few hours at the airport, and she had seen practically nothing of the place, contenting herself with buying lots of postcards and souvenirs for her friends back home.

The journey itself was accomplished remarkably easily. Debra had felt concerned about Dominic McGill's presence, but she needn't have worried. They were also accompanied by Steve Lanni, Aaron's personal assistant, and another man called Victor Ross, who was Dominic's secretary, and also a close friend. In consequence, Debra sat with Aaron and Steve Lanni, and saw little of McGill at all. At first, the opulence of their accommodation on the aircraft was sufficient to hold her interest, but after a while she fell back on the many magazines which the stewardess had provided her with, flicking through them carelessly, anxiously anticipating their arrival at the house of her aunt in Valleydown. Aunt Julia would not be pleased, particularly if this all turned out to be a mistake, for she hated unexpected company at any time, and Debra knew she would feel the whiplash of her aunt's tongue once the visitors had left.

Again and again she pondered on the problem. Why, if it were true, had Aunt Julia never told her, never revealed her parentage? What secrets had been kept from her all these years? And how could anyone keep such a secret without feeling any sense of conspiracy and guilt?

New York was a huge bustling metropolis, jammed with cars and buses, and full of people all of whom seemed in a desperate hurry to get to their destinations. Debra felt lost and confused, unable to cope with the traffic, the crowds and the noise. In comparison, London seemed warm and confined and familiar. But she ascended the heights of the Empire State Building, and watched the ducks in Central Park, as well as walking with Aaron along the fabulous shopping area, Madison Avenue. Aaron insisted on buying her a royal blue velvet slack suit which she admired in a shop window, and when she came out after trying it on, he smiled satisfactorily and said:

'Darling, you must get used to me buying you things. I'd like to give you everything you've ever dreamed of, if you'll let me.'

Debra shook her head, sighing. 'Oh, Aaron,' she said, hugging his arm involuntarily. 'You make me feel so warm and secure that I'm afraid.'

'Afraid of what?'

She lifted her shoulders helplessly. 'I don't know. Maybe that we'll find it's all a dream, and then....'

Aaron studied her expression. 'This aunt of yours, she's not exactly coming through to me as a sympathetic character.'

Debra bit her lip. 'I'm being less than kind.' She

frowned. 'After all, it can't have been easy for her, looking after me the way she has. I mean, whatever her reasons, she has done her best for me.'

'Has she? I wonder.'

Debra's eyes were troubled. 'At least she didn't abandon me at birth,' she said quietly. 'I mean, if I am Elizabeth Steel's daughter, that's what she did, didn't she?'

Aaron inclined his head slowly. 'We shall soon know,' he said dryly.

The skies of London were dark and hung with clouds, and a faint drizzle was falling, when the huge aircraft landed at twelve midnight. Customs formalities were soon over, and then they were out in the large reception area of the air terminal, and porters were taking their luggage to a waiting limousine. The car, a sleek black Mercedes, was chauffeured by a small, dapper man in his fifties, who greeted both Aaron and Dominic with obvious pleasure and led the way to the automobile chatting about the terrible weather, and their trip, just as though it was midday instead of the middle of the night.

In the car Debra was seated in the back between Aaron and Steve Lanni, who was a man of Aaron's age, and whom she had grown to like very much. Victor Ross and Dominic both sat in front with Potter, the chauffeur.

A suite had been booked for them at the Hilton, but Debra was too tired to take any real notice of her surroundings. She was shown to her room, and after refusing the services of a maid to do her unpacking for her, she merely showered in the exquisitely appointed bathroom, unpacked her nightdress, and slid between the soft sheets of the bed. She was exhausted, which was just as well, for it removed the anxieties of the trip and its outcome from her mind completely.

The next morning when she awoke, she couldn't, for a moment, remember where she was. The heavy yellow curtains hanging at the windows, the creamy thick carpet on the floor, the smooth satin of the honey-coloured bedspread, were all unfamiliar to her. And then it all came flooding back, and she sighed, and rolling over consulted her wristwatch which she had placed on the table beside the bed the night before. She blinked rapidly when she read its dial; it could not possibly be right: twelve-fifteen!

She slid out of bed and ran to the window. She could see the wide expanse of Hyde Park away to the right, while the traffic converging on the road outside proved that it was indeed midday, and she had slept for practically twelve hours. It was unbelievable, and she wondered what the others were doing, and whether they had gone out without her.

She hastily washed, and dressed in the orange suit which she had worn the previous day. It was her only good suit, and was the most formal thing she possessed. She toyed with the idea of wearing the new slack suit, but then discarded it. Much as she knew the suit looked good on her, it was not the kind of wearing apparel likely to appeal to Aunt Julia's severe eyes.

When she emerged into the adjoining lounge she found Victor Ross sprawled lazily on a comfortable red leather couch, reading the newspapers.

'Hi,' he greeted her, smiling. 'So you finally came to. I was beginning to get worried.'

Debra blushed, and smiled, too. 'I have overslept,' she admitted awkwardly. 'What must Aaron think of me?'

'Aaron, Dominic and Steve left a couple of hours ago,' remarked Victor, sitting up and fastening his collar button. He tightened the knot of his tie and rose to his feet reluctantly. 'I guess they'll be back in an hour. Meanwhile, I suggest we have some lunch.'

Debra smoothed her hair back behind her small ears. 'I always seem to be left as someone's responsibility,' she said, shrugging. 'I mean, I do know London rather well, and I'm perfectly capable of taking myself to lunch and being back here in an hour.'

Victor's grin widened. 'Honey, why should you suppose I don't want to take you to lunch? Believe me, I don't mind at all.'

'You're being very polite, but——'

'But nothing! Hell, you're one attractive dame, and no one can say that Victor Ross doesn't like an attractive dame.'

Debra laughed. 'All right, I'll take your word for it. You're very kind.'

'Kind nothing. I shall enjoy it.'

They ate in the hotel restaurant, and during the meal Debra found she could talk to Victor quite freely. Up until then they had barely exchanged two words together, but all at once they got to know each other very well indeed. She relaxed in his company, and listened with interest when he talked about his work with Dominic McGill, and the various countries they had visited in their search for material for Dominic's writing talents.

'I guess I've known Dominic all my life,' he said reminiscently. 'We grew up together, in the same rough neighbourhood.'

'Where was that?' asked Debra, accepting a cigarette from him.

'Brooklyn. Some life we had! I guess it's hard for you to believe now, looking at Dom, and all the things he has. But it hasn't always been easy, believe me! Only his driving ambition brought him to the brink of success.'

'Are ... are his parents still alive?'

'Nope. His old lady died two, three years back. I guess he never knew his father.'

'I see.' Debra bent her head, remembering the day Dominic had taken her to see Elizabeth Steel's hacienda near San José. She had talked about illegitimacy then, and he had seemed amused at her attempts to justify herself. She had told him he knew nothing about it, and she felt contrite. It was true what he had said, there could be no stigma attached to a new-born child, an innocent being brought into the world without any voluntary act on its part.

Victor was looking at her. 'What's wrong? Have I shocked you?' He grimaced. 'Why, in our neighbourhood there were kids without any parents. We considered ourselves lucky because we had homes to go to, even if they were awful places.'

'You haven't shocked me,' replied Debra seriously. 'No, I was just thinking, that's all. Tell me about how Dominic became successful.'

Victor shrugged. 'Hasn't he told you?'

'If he had, I wouldn't be asking.'

'That's true.' Victor studied the glowing tip of his cigarette. 'Well, I guess you could say Elizabeth Steel was responsible.'

'I see.' Debra felt her nerves tighten. 'How?'

'Oh, I guess she persuaded Aaron to look at his play.' Victor halted. 'Look, say, this isn't really my affair. I'd ... I'd rather you asked Dom yourself.'

Debra frowned. 'Why? What's so secret? I know that Dominic knew Elizabeth Steel very well. Aaron has told me that.'

Victor looked across the restaurant, biting his lips thoughtfully. Then he brightened. 'Well, I guess we don't have any more time right now. Here comes Dom.'

Debra stifled the sense of frustration she felt. She

was becoming far too interested in Dominic McGill's affairs. The sooner she put him out of her thoughts, the better it would be.

Dominic McGill halted at their table, and Debra glanced up at him. Dressed today in a dark brown suit, a cream shirt, and mushroom-coloured tie, which just showed above the top buttons of his waistcoat, he looked very attractive, and half the restaurant was looking his way.

'Hi,' he said, enveloping them both in his gaze. 'I guess you slept well, Debra.'

Debra felt her cheeks burn. 'Y . . . yes, thank you.'

'Good. Have you had lunch?'

Victor answered. 'Just finished. Have you?'

'Well, we grabbed a sandwich at the studio,' replied Dominic, grinning. 'I should think I can survive until dinner. Do you want another drink?'

'No, thank you,' replied Debra at once, and Victor shook his head.

'Not right now. Where are Aaron and Steve?'

'Waiting in the bar. If you're ready, we can go.'

'Are . . . are we going to Valleydown now?' asked Debra unsteadily.

'Sure.'

'Then I'll get my things.'

'Why?' Dominic frowned. 'You won't be staying.'

'I . . . I . . . of course I will. I mean, even if this is true, Valleydown is my home.'

'Aaron's instructions, not mine,' remarked Dominic sardonically. 'Come on, let's go.'

Debra stood up angrily. 'I'll get my case,' she said pointedly.

'Okay, okay, get your case,' muttered Dominic, looking bored by the whole argument. 'If you must insist on behaving like a child!'

Victor stood up too, and looked from one to the

other of them thoughtfully. 'Come on, Dom, let's get a drink,' he said, walking towards the restaurant door.

'Yeah, let's,' Dominic gave Debra a final sardonic glance, then followed her as she stormed away across the room.

When she had collected all her things together, Debra opened her room door to find a porter waiting to take her suitcases down for her. She presumed that either Dominic or Victor had sent him up and she compressed her lips impatiently. Then, sighing, she handed over the cases and followed him along to the lift.

Aaron was waiting in reception, and frowned when he saw the cases.

'Debra, don't you trust me?' he asked reproachfully. 'Couldn't you at least have given me the chance to spend a little time with you, even if this isn't true? I mean, you do look like Elizabeth, and I gain great pleasure from being with you.'

Debra flushed. 'I'm sorry, Aaron. But whatever happens, I ought to stay with Aunt Julia.'

Aaron sighed. 'All right, all right. We'll see what happens. But you must promise me that if anything goes wrong, and I've left, then you'll come to me before anyone else.'

'Aaron!' Debra took his arm. 'You really are making me feel terrible. The trouble is, I want to stay with you, I like being with you, and that frightens me, you see. I mustn't allow myself to become so involved.'

'Darling, you are involved,' said Aaron, leading the way out to the Mercedes. 'Whatever happens now, I shan't be able to forget you, and I doubt whether you will forget either.'

'I know. That's what bothers me,' said Debra, feeling her stomach contract at the sight of Dominic McGill standing outside on the hotel steps.

But to her surprise, McGill was not travelling with them. Only she and Aaron and Steve Lanni went in the Mercedes. Victor Ross and Dominic climbed into a cream-coloured Jensen, and with Dominic at the wheel sped away before Potter could get behind the wheel of the Mercedes. Debra felt a twinge of envy that they should travel at such speed when Potter drove very sedately, and she had to chide herself for again associating Dominic McGill with herself.

Valleydown lay in a fold of the downs as its name suggested, and from the hill above the small town could be seen the faint line of the coast. It was a dull June day, suggestive of a storm, and Debra wondered if it was an ominous indication of the storm that was to come.

'I ... I'd like to speak to my aunt alone first,' she said, as they began the sweep down into Valleydown's main street.

Aaron looked at her thoughtfully. 'I don't know about that,' he said, frowning. 'I would like to be with you.'

'Aaron, she's going to get a terrible shock, whatever way we put it. At least let me do it my way.'

Aaron hesitated, then shrugged. 'Very well. I can't force you, of course. I just wish you would realise that this aunt of yours may not crack as easily as you think.'

'She is my aunt,' said Debra quietly. 'And I don't want to hurt her more than I can help.'

'All right, so be it. Potter, stop in the town centre. We're bound to come upon Dominic there.'

'Yes, Mr. Johannson.'

Potter turned into the market place, and immediately they could see the cream Jensen, parked in the small parking area, with Victor and Dominic leaning against its bonnet, smoking.

'Well,' said Aaron, 'this is where we part company, if

that's really what you want.'

'It's really what I want,' said Debra. 'You ... you know the address, don't you?'

'Yes, seventeen River Walk. I imagine it's easy enough to find.'

'Anyone will tell you where to go,' nodded Debra, sliding out of the luxurious automobile with a strange kind of reluctance. 'Give me half an hour alone with her, and then you can come.'

Dominic came strolling over. 'What gives?'

Aaron climbed out of the Mercedes. 'Debra wants to go and see her aunt alone first. I've agreed. We follow on later.'

'Is is far from here?' asked Dominic.

'No, not very,' replied Debra, not looking at him.

'Come on. I'll give you a lift,' said Dominic easily.

'That's not necessary.'

'Don't be so damned independent!' exclaimed Aaron. 'Let Dom at least take you to the end of the block.'

Debra shrugged. 'All right. But it's not far.'

The cream Jensen was smooth and comfortable. Dominic glanced at her questioningly, then said:

'Are you scared?'

Debra swallowed hard. 'A little.'

He turned the car into River Drive, at her direction, the road which led into River Walk. His hands slid expertly round the wheel, and she wished impulsively that he was going to be with her. She didn't know why, but she felt more secure with him suddenly than she did with Aaron.

As though sensing her uncertainty, he looked her way again. 'Are you sure you want to go through with this alone?' he murmured. 'I guess I'm prepared to brave Aaron's wrath and come with you now.'

Debra hesitated only momentarily, then shook her

head. 'I . . . I'd like to say yes,' she said honestly. 'But I can't. This is my problem, not yours.'

'Okay. Is this it?' He halted the car.

'Yes.' Debra opened her door and slid out. 'Thank you for bringing me, anyway.'

His eyes were gentle for once, and she felt suddenly breathless. Then she turned away abruptly, and began to walk along past the narrow houses of River Walk.

Debra rang the bell before entering the house even though she had her own key. She did not want to upset her aunt unnecessarily, and Aunt Julia would be bound to be astounded to see her back in England so suddenly.

Everything was the same; the same grey carpet in the hall, the same mahogany hallstand, the same brown paint on the doors. Debra shut the front door and leaned back against it, putting off the moment when she would face her aunt. There was a tight constriction in her throat, and she fumbled for her handbag in search of a cigarette. At that moment Julia Warren emerged from the kitchen, on her way to answer the door, and when she saw Debra her expression was one of astonished disbelief.

'Debra!' she exclaimed. 'But how can this be? It's not a week since I had your last letter and you never mentioned anything about coming home.'

Then she noticed the girl's pale cheeks, and her grey eyes narrowed. Debra stared at her, and then straightening up from her position against the door, she walked slowly down the dark hallway.

'I . . . I've come home because something has happened,' she said, swallowing hard. 'Something I've just got to talk to you about.'

Julia Warren's features tightened. 'Is that so?'

'Yes.' Debra reached her aunt. 'Can we go into the living room? We can't talk here.'

Julia shrugged, and pushed open the living-room door, watching Debra strangely. There was a kind of guarded look in her eyes, and Debra felt her strength draining away from her. How could she broach such a subject? How could she ask her aunt a thing so ... so ... *damning*?

In the living room, Debra stood with her back to the fireplace, empty now even though it was a cool day. She took out her cigarettes and lit one, waiting for Aunt Julia's usual remonstrations, but they did not come. Julia Warren made no comment, but merely stood with her arms folded over her aproned chest. Debra studied her as she lit the cigarette, seeing the hard features she had known all her life, the iron-grey hair drawn into a knot, trying to find some resemblance between Julia and the photograph she had seen of Elizabeth Steel. It was difficult, and yet there was an indefinable something that made Debra's stomach sink to its lowest point.

She ran a tongue over her dry lips, trying to find words to say what was uppermost in her mind, but no words would come. Instead, she felt the pricking pain of tears behind her eyes, and bent her head, furious with herself for behaving so emotionally. Then Julia Warren spoke.

'You've found out, haven't you?' she said, in an expressionless voice. 'Or at least you suspect!'

Debra stared at her, a hand to her throat. 'Wh ... what do you think I've found out, Aunt Julia?'

'That you are Elizabeth Steel's daughter,' replied Aunt Julia, her eyes cold and full of dislike. 'I knew I ought never to have let you go to America. But God help me, I thought the chances of your finding out were so minimal as to be practically non-existent. How did it happen?'

'Wait!' Debra shook her head. 'Don't ask me that.

Tell me! I ... I *am* Elizabeth Steel's daughter?'

Julia Warren shrugged. 'Yes, you're her daughter.'

'But ... but ..!' Debra bit her lip. 'Oh, *God!*' and she burst into tears.

Julia Warren watched her dispassionately. Debra felt dizzy and sick, and sank down on to a low chair, trying to control herself.

'Calm yourself,' said Julia, not moving from her position, making no move to comfort the girl. 'How much do you know? Any of it?'

Debra shook her head, dried her eyes and tried to remain calm. 'I ... I don't know. I've met ... Aaron ... Aaron Johannson. He ... he told me you might be Elizabeth's sister. Are you?'

'Yes, I'm her sister. More's the pity!'

'Why?' Debra looked up. 'Why? And why didn't you tell *me*?

Julia snorted angrily. 'What was there to tell you? That your mother was little more than a harlot——'

'Oh no!'

'Oh, yes.' Now Julia Warren was animated. 'What do you want to know, Debra? Would you like to know who your father was? Is that it?'

Debra shivered at the hatred in her voice. 'Aunt Julia——'

'No, be quiet! All right, I'll tell you. All of it! All the messy, horrible business!'

'Please, Aunt Julia,' began Debra, 'don't be like this. Why do you hate my mother so much?'

Julia strode angrily across the room, standing over Debra and looking down at her with hard eyes. 'I'll tell you why I hate your mother,' she almost spat the words. 'Your *mother* stole my *husband!* Oh, yes, that surprises you, doesn't it? You never knew I ever had a husband, did you?'

Debra shook her head, in blind dismay.

'No, well, I did! When Elizabeth ran away to the States to make a name for herself, I stayed home and married a man, a decent man, or so I foolishly imagined.'

'Oh, no!' Debra was trembling now.

'Oh, yes. And of course, after Elizabeth became famous, she came over to see us on a flying visit. She had left her husband at home. Yes, she had a husband, too, or do you already know that?'

Debra nodded.

'Yes, well, she had left poor, harmless Aaron at home. She only married him because she thought he would be useful to her. She never bothered with anybody unless they were useful to her. That shocks you, doesn't it? But your mother was no saint, so never think she was. Well, she came to see Arnold and me. We hadn't been married long, and Arnold was an attractive man.' Julia gave a mirthless laugh. 'Elizabeth could never leave any attractive man alone for long. I leave you to guess what happened. . . . She could do nothing in America without Aaron finding out, so she came to me. To *me*!' Julia at last seemed emotionally disturbed. 'Imagine *that*! Coming to me! I didn't believe her at first, but then Arnold—Oh, God! It was awful!'

'Oh, no!' Debra was crying softly now, her fingers over her ears.

'Oh, yes. That was your dear mother all over. She didn't give a damn what happened to Arnold and me, so long as no one found out. At first I refused to have anything to do with it, but then Elizabeth threatened to make the story public. I didn't believe she'd do it, it would have been worse for her than for me, but I couldn't take the chance. I'm no gambler. So I told her she could stay until the baby was born, and then once it was here I would pretend it was my baby, and she must go away and never come back.'

Debra raised her face. 'And she did *that*!'

'Yes. We moved away from the flat we had had when the baby was due, and Elizabeth returned to the States.' She bent her head, and Debra thought for a moment she was crying, but there was only a frustrated expression on her face. 'You would think nothing more could happen,' she said slowly. 'But we hadn't considered my husband's feelings in all this. While Elizabeth lived with us he was like a man possessed. There was no approaching him, and I really believe he hated her as much as I did. But then, then ... after the baby was born, you, that is, and Elizabeth had gone, he became morose and depressed, and I couldn't get through to him. I realise now that he loved your mother all the time. Two months after she had gone, he stepped absentmindedly into the road in front of a bus. He never recovered consciousness.'

'Oh, *no*!' Debra felt the blood running chill through her veins. In all her vain imaginings, she had thought of nothing like this.

Julia sighed heavily, then straightened her shoulders. 'When Elizabeth heard of Arnold's death she came back. She had changed, too, and she wanted *you*. *You*, the only bit of Arnold left belonging to me!'

Debra looked up. 'And what happened?

'I'll tell you what happened. She didn't get you. Did she imagine I would allow her to take you when she had taken everything else I had? No, I told her if she ever came to see you again I would expose her, tell everything. There was always the birth certificate, you see, made out in her real name of Elizabeth Morrison. Warren was your father's name, so naturally it's yours too.'

'But she did want me,' murmured Debra faintly.

'Yes, she wanted you. She realized what she'd given

95

away then. She even said she was willing to tell Aaron the truth. But Aaron was only a small part of it. If the story had been publicized in the way I threatened it would be, her career would have been ruined. Can you imagine the headlines: *Famous Actress's Affair with Sister's Husband!*'

'Stop it, stop it!' Debra pressed trembling hands to her mouth. 'It's awful, *awful!*'

'So you see, I kept the truth from you, as much for your sake as for my own.'

Debra shook her head. 'It's ... it's too much. I can't take it in.'

'Why? What did you believe? Come to think of it, what did Aaron Johannson believe? That you might conceivably be his daughter? That's a laugh!'

Debra shook her head. 'Don't be so cruel,' she said unsteadily. 'Aaron is a wonderful man. He's been very kind to me.'

'A wonderful man!' scoffed her aunt unkindly. 'I wonder if he'll be so wonderful when he knows the truth!'

'That's enough!'

Both women started at the unexpected command, and Julia Warren spun round to face the man who was now standing in the doorway of the living room, his hard blue eyes cold as he looked at her.

'What do you think you're doing?' she exclaimed, and then spun back round to face Debra who had risen unsteadily to her feet. 'Who is this man? How dare he walk into my house like this? I thought you came in alone!'

'So she did,' said Dominic McGill, before Debra could speak. 'But I couldn't leave her to face it alone, and by God, I'm glad I didn't. Knowing Debra as I think I do, she would never have relayed this story to Aaron.'

96

'How ... how long have you been there?' asked Debra shakily.

'Long enough,' replied Dominic, studying her tear-stained features. 'But I couldn't interrupt before this. I had to know the whole story.'

Julia Warren gripped her niece's shoulders angrily. 'Who is this man? Tell me!'

'He ... he's Dominic McGill,' said Debra nervously. 'He's ... he's a playwright and film writer.'

Julia released her and swung back to Dominic. 'Oh, yes, I've heard of you,' she acceded grudgingly. 'Another of Elizabeth's satellites, I suppose.'

'You could say that,' remarked Dominic, his voice cold. He looked at Debra. 'You realise, I guess, that the story you've heard is only one side of the story, and naturally a biased one.'

Debra was shivering uncontrollably, and with a muffled exclamation Dominic crossed the space between them and pulled her into his arms. Debra felt the hot tears burning her cheeks, wetting his suit front, but when she tried to draw back he muttered:

'Relax, kid, you've had enough for one afternoon.' He looked at Julia Warren. 'I guess you're satisfied now,' he said savagely. 'You've had your revenge, haven't you? What were you waiting for, I wonder? You eventually intended telling her the truth, didn't you? After all, she is Elizabeth's child, isn't she?'

'She is also Arnold's child,' retorted Julia furiously, her face contorted with rage. 'How dare you speak to me like that! You're just as bad as she was, only concerned with your own selfish desires.'

'Whatever else Elizabeth was, she wasn't selfish,' said Dominic harshly. 'Okay, she was ambitious, we all are in our own little ways, and I guess what she did to you was wrong. But remember, it takes two to commit the act of love, and your sainted husband was no better

97

than she was, or no worse!'

Julia clenched her fists. 'Shut up, damn you, you know nothing about it.'

'I knew Elizabeth,' he retorted coldly. 'And I also know she was basically a generous and loving creature. Aaron knew what he was doing when he married her, he had no illusions that she was in love with him.'

Debra struggled back a little and looked up at him. 'Aaron said you didn't know they were married.'

'Hell, of course I knew. Elizabeth told me herself. But that's beside the point, surely. What is true is that Elizabeth loved this Arnold Warren for a period in time, and he loved her. You are the result of that love, not the sordid tragedy that this co-called aunt of yours is making it out to be.' He shook his head. 'And knowing Elizabeth as I did, I can't believe she would abandon you without making certain that you would be well cared for. Remember, she thought she was leaving you with your father, and when he was killed she tried to get you back. Your aunt has a lot to answer for. Okay, I can see her point of view, she was lonely and embittered, but when Elizabeth wanted to see you, she denied her that right. Remember her words: *I told her if she tried to see you again, I would expose her.* Are those the words of a woman without envy or hatred?'

Debra drew away from him reluctantly. She felt weak and confused, and she felt she needed time to think, time to assimilate the events of the last few minutes.

'So where does that leave me?' she whispered achingly.

Julia Warren sneered, 'It leaves you as the unwanted child of an illicit liaison!'

Dominic looked at her, an expression of loathing upon his face. 'Don't ever say that again,' he muttered, 'or I might forget that I'm supposed to be a gentleman, I've never hit a woman yet, but there's always a first time.'

Julia hunched her shoulders. 'It's all a game to you,' she said, breathing rapidly, with suppressed anger. 'It was my life Elizabeth ruined.'

Debra nodded her head. 'Yes, that's true, Dominic, that's *true!*' She used his name involuntarily, without noticing she had done so.

Dominic moved restlessly. 'So what! Debra, this kind of thing happens every day. I'm not condoning it, but is that any reason to stop you from living the life you were entitled to lead?'

'I don't know. I don't *know!*' Debra was beginning to sound hysterical, and Dominic decided it was time for him to take charge of the situation.

'Look,' he said, 'I guess it takes time to understand a thing like this. You can't possibly take it all in at once. I realise that.'

Julia looked at him. 'So what do you suggest she does?' she asked sarcastically.

'I suggest she comes back to London with us, Aaron and me. Oh, yes, Aaron's here.' He glanced at his watch. 'He should be ringing your bell any minute now. But I don't think there's anything useful to be achieved by staying here and relaying all that has happened. I can tell Aaron myself.'

'This is Debra's home,' snapped Julia. 'I won't let her go.'

'You can't stop her,' retorted Dominic coldly. 'And I'm not leaving without her.'

'No, Dominic, no ... I'll stay,' began Debra quietly.

'Like hell you will,' he swore furiously.

'So she leaves with you and gets your biased opinion instead of mine,' exclaimed Julia hotly.

'My opinion is not as biased as yours, or as cruel,' he

retorted. 'You want to kill her spirit, subdue her, as you could never subdue Elizabeth, isn't that right?'

'This is Debra's home,' she repeated. 'If she leaves here with you, I'll never take her back again, *ever*.'

'Oh, Aunt Julia,' began Debra, biting her lips, 'don't be like this! *Please!*'

'If you stay here it will be on my terms,' said Julia. 'Put all this out of your mind. Remember, we have lived together for twenty-two years. Can you change in the course of thirty minutes the habits of a lifetime?'

'Aunt Julia——'

'Shut up!' Julia was still furiously angry.

'Yes, stop it,' said Dominic, running a hand over his hair restively. 'Debra, think carefully before you commit yourself.'

Debra sighed, 'It's like you said. I need time. *Time!*'

'Well, I'm not giving you any time,' said Julia. 'In fact I don't particularly care what you do. You're not the same girl that went away. And I don't think I know you any more.'

'Oh, Aunt Julia!' Debra stared at her wide-eyed. 'You don't mean that!'

'Don't I? Don't you believe it! You're changing already. Go with this man, and much good may it do you. But don't come running to me when your pretty little world falls to pieces!'

Debra was horrified. If she had thought she knew her aunt, she had been very much mistaken. This bitter, spiteful woman could think of nothing but her own hatred for her sister. A hatred engendered by goodness knew what events in the past. Events that Debra could never hope to understand.

Dominic waited no longer, but took Debra's arm and hustled her to the door. Debra looked back at Aunt Julia, still praying for a miracle to happen, something that would wipe away all the pain and hurt that her aunt had inflicted, but Julia Warren merely turned away, and the last Debra saw of her was the rigid, unyielding stiffness of her narrow back.

Debra lay listlessly on her bed in the London hotel. For the moment she felt numb, drained of all emotion, and completely incapable of deciding what she was going to do with her life. She refused to think of that terrible scene in the house in River Walk, even though it still lay in the back of her mind, just waiting to torment her. She felt as though it was all some horrible nightmare, and when she had emerged from the house she had felt depression sweeping down upon her without any sign of relief.

Aaron Johannson had been about to get out of his car at the gate when she and Dominic had left the house, but at Dominic's curt gesture had remained in his seat and indicated to Potter to drive on. Dominic had put Debra firmly into the front seat of the Jensen, and then walked quickly round the bonnet to slide in beside her. He had not spoken to her, leaving her to the silence she craved, only switching on the radio very low so that the soft music relaxed her, and relieved the taut atmosphere.

Debra had felt so grateful to him, not only for extricating her from an impossible situation, but also for being there, for sharing it with her, and for being able therefore to relay the truth to Aaron, because as he had said she was sure she would never have been able to do so.

They had driven straight back to the hotel, over-taking the Mercedes on the way, and once there he had seen her to her room and left her. And now here she was, lying in the stillness of her room feeling completely alone for the first time in her life.

She lit a cigarette and blew smoke rings towards the

ceiling, trying to think coherently. What, in actual fact, was to become of her? She no longer had a home to go to, no job, at least not for several months yet in Valleydown, and anyhow, how could she return there *now*? She rolled on to her stomach. It would be so easy to give way to self-pity, she thought tiredly. She just wanted to cry and cry, and she was determined not to do so. She had cried enough already, and crying solved nothing. She traced the pattern of the bedspread with her finger, wondering whether Dominic had told Aaron the truth yet. And when he did, what would Aaron say? That tantalising sense of belonging she had felt in his presence had merely been wishful thinking. Maybe—maybe he would hate her now, like her aunt did. After all, he had been betrayed just as much as Aunt Julia.

She rolled back on to her back, biting her lips to stop them from trembling. Oh God, she thought, I couldn't bear another scene like that one with Aunt Julia.

She was unaware and uncaring of the fact that her face was now completely bare of make-up, and her hair was all mussed from lying on the bed, and when there was a knock at the door she called 'Come in,' carelessly.

She sat up with a start when she saw that it was Dominic. She ran a hand over her hair, trying to smooth it, and pushed her feet into her shoes. He closed the door and leaned back against it, studying her.

'Relax,' he said, lighting a cigarette. 'How do you feel?'

'All ... all right, thank you.' She ran a hand down her cheek. 'I ... I must look a mess.'

He shook his head. 'No, just tousled, that's all,' he replied, smiling. 'I like it. You look like a schoolgirl.'

Debra flushed. 'Do I? I ... I'm not sure that's a compliment.' She was trying to act naturally, but she failed abysmally when her voice broke.

Dominic straightened, and came across to the bed and seated himself beside her, legs apart, his hands hanging loosely between. Then he looked wryly at her.

'I guess it's been quite a day, hasn't it?' he murmured.

Debra nodded, looking down at her toes, not trusting herself to speak.

'Never mind, it's over now. Things can only get better, not worse.'

Debra shrugged. 'I wouldn't bank on that. Ha ... have you told Aaron?'

'Yes.'

'And ... wh ... what did he say?'

Dominic smiled, touching her cheek gently. 'What did you think he would say?'

Debra shivered, not so much from the thought of what Aaron might have said as from the touch of Dominic's hand. It had an electrifying effect on her, and she wondered wildly why he should affect her in such a way.

'I ... I don't know. Was he ... was he angry?'

'Yes.'

'Oh!' Debra stared at him with wide eyes.

Dominic shook his head impatiently. 'Oh, not mad in the way you mean! Mad because this aunt of yours treated you like she did!'

'But ... I mean....' Debra halted. 'What about my ... my father? I mean ... he thought I might be ... I mean .. oh, you *know* what I mean!'

'Sure I do. But Aaron's not small-minded. Baby, for him you're the reincarnation of Elizabeth Steel, and the fact that you're her daughter is just a bonus. Besides, he likes you, he really does, and as Elizabeth was married to him when she had you, I guess that makes you some relation.'

Debra stood up and walked across to the window, looking down unseeingly on the street below.

'You ... you wouldn't be fooling me, would you?' she said, in a tight little voice.

'Why should I do that? No, honey, I'm serious. Aaron believes you are like Elizabeth in every way, and to him, now that it's been proved, it means one thing: you must have her talent as well as her looks.'

'Oh no!' Debra swung round. 'No! I'm no actress.'

Dominic rose to his feet and walked across to her where she was leaning against the wall by the window, and put one hand against the wall on either side of her, studying her at close quarters. Debra felt suddenly breathless. He was so close she could see every line of his face, the curling length of his lashes, the whiteness of his teeth, even smell the indefinable male scent about him. She wanted to move closer to him, press herself against his lean, hard body, feel those arms close about her and that hard mouth against her own. She wanted to run her fingers through his hair where it grew down his neck to the collar of his shirt, and never let him go.

'How do you know you're no good?' he asked now, compelling her to control her crazy thoughts. 'You made a good test. Emmet was well pleased with you. You have done some amateur dramatics, haven't you?'

'O ... only at school,' she stammered, compressing her lips.

'So! Aaron can make you a star. It's what he wants to do. Let him do it! You've nothing else to do.'

'No!' Debra bent her head, twisting her hands nervously. 'I ... I can't go back to the States. I'm English, this is my home!'

'You have no home, not now,' he said insistently. 'Debra, look at me, *listen* to me! For God's sake don't

104

throw it all away, not now. It should have been your birthright.'

Debra shook her head, still not looking at him, and he swore softly. 'Debra, Debra, what is it you're afraid of? Where's the harm? Aaron won't hurt you, I can guarantee you that. And he's not a young man any more. You would give him a great deal of delight and happiness. Can you deny him, or yourself, the chance for happiness?'

'I ... I don't know. I don't know anything any more.' She looked into his eyes at last. 'I feel lost ... and alone.'

'There's no reason to feel lost or alone,' he said softly. 'Back home in California, you'll have a hell of a time! Baby, you just haven't begun to live yet! And the men will all fall flat on their faces!' he grinned.

'Oh, Dominic!' Debra shook her head again. 'You make it sound so *easy*!'

'It is easy. Where's the difficulty? Aaron can arrange all the details for you, all you've got to do is agree.'

'But I don't want to be a film star.'

'How do you know?'

Debra sighed. 'Oh, I don't know, I just do. I'm not cut out for press photographers and gossip columnists and star treatment. I would never have time for the things I want to do.'

'And what do you want to do?'

'Well—reading, listening to music, any number of things.'

He laughed softly. 'Oh, you really are unique, honey, you really are. Here you are being offered the earth, and you're asking for one of the islands in the Pacific!'

Debra smiled at his metaphors. 'Well, I'm just me,' she said. 'But you're right in one respect. There's no one else who gives a damn about me.'

'Stop feeling sorry for yourself,' he said, frowning. 'Relax and enjoy life a little. You'll see, when you've half a dozen boy-friends in tow you won't even stop to consider the consequences.'

Debra clenched her fists. 'Will you stop treating me like a teenager to be humoured!' she exclaimed hotly.

He grinned, 'That's better. Now that was more like the Debra Warren I used to know. As for treating you like a teenager, when you stop acting like one, I'll stop treating you like one!'

Debra glared at him angrily, hating the mocking lift of his mouth. He was so cool and confident, so assured and sophisticated and detached, and it infuriated her. He ought not to be so impersonal, when by standing close to her like this he was disturbing her both physically and mentally. She wanted to wipe the sarcasm from his attractive face, make him aware of her as she was of him.

'Why do you think I act like a teenager?' she stormed at him. 'Because I'm not trying to flirt with you all the time; because I don't respond to your obvious sexual appeal?'

His eyes narrowed and she felt a sense of satisfaction that at last she had roused him. Pressing home her advantage, she continued:

'Do you think I'm too inexperienced and naive to know about men? Is that it? The small-town schoolmistress without any sex appeal!'

'I didn't say that,' he remarked coldly. 'What is this? A way of working out your frustration?'

Debra flushed miserably. She had only succeeded in making him angry, and probably regard her as even more childish than he thought before.

'Well,' she said, 'you're talking of me having boy-friends as though I'd never had one before.'

'And have you?' he asked coolly.

Debra bent her head. 'Of course I have.'

'Really?' He sounded sceptical.

'Yes, really!' Her eyes were still stormy.

'So you consider you know all about it, is that it?' he asked lazily.

Debra shrugged. 'There's not much to know, is there?'

'That's a matter of opinion,' he smiled, mocking her again.

Debra turned away suddenly, unable to stand any more of this verbal sparring. Dominic straightened, put his hands into his trousers pockets and walked towards the door. 'By the way, Aaron asked me to tell you he's expecting you to join him for dinner.' He glanced at his watch. 'It's already seven-fifteen, and dinner is at eight, so you'd better speed up, honey.'

Debra did not answer, and shrugging, he went out of the room.

Debra showered and dressed for dinner without any enthusiasm. She dreaded meeting Dominic again, feeling that she had behaved abominably considering how kind he had been to her all day. She didn't know what was the matter with her; she had never acted like that before. She wore the midnight blue crocheted lace dress, which was her only alternative to the black, and left her hair loose about her shoulders. She wondered whether she would ever have the courage to return to Valleydown for the rest of her things. There were other items, more important than clothes, like several books and records she valued, and she was loath to relinquish everything she had possessed.

When she emerged into the lounge of the suite, she found Aaron waiting for her alone. She glanced round questioningly, and he said:

'There is only to be the two of us. Dominic and

107

Victor are dining with friends, and Steve is catching up on some work.'

'Oh, I see.' Debra ran a tongue over her dry lips. 'Well, I'm ready. Shall we go?'

'Of course. I took the liberty of booking a table for us at Mandini's. It's a small restaurant I frequent when I'm in London, and the food is very good.'

Even Aaron sounded slightly tense, and Debra preceded him out of the room without making any further comment.

Mandini's was small, as Aaron had said, but it was obviously a very expensive restaurant, and from the way Aaron was deferred to by the waiters, he was a valued client. They were given a table in an alcove, near the small dais on which a three-piece group was playing. The music was low and unobtrusive, the willowy strains of a reed pipe blending rhythmically with a guitar and organ.

Aaron ordered Martini cocktails, and then took charge of the menu, after Debra had suggested that he choose for her. They began with prawn cocktail, progressed to an enormous mixed grill, and had strawberry mousse to follow. They didn't speak much during the meal except to comment on the various dishes and Debra was beginning to wonder whether Dominic had been a little optimistic in his estimate of Aaron's feelings. Maybe he had changed his mind about her, just as her aunt had done.

Then, when the coffee was served, and Debra had refused a liqueur, he said: 'Now, let's talk about you, and your future.'

Debra accepted a cigarette from him, running a tongue over her dry lips. 'What about my future?' she murmured questioningly.

Aaron frowned. 'Didn't Dominic explain?'

Debra shook her head. 'I don't know. I suppose he

did in a way, but I can't believe you want me, not *me*. You want a facsimile of Elizabeth Steel. I don't want to be someone's double, I want to be me, Debra Warren!' She sighed, looking down at her cigarette. 'I'm sorry. I seem to be disappointing you from all angles.'

Aaron's fingers gripped her hand. 'Don't say that, Debra, don't ever say that!' His voice was harsh. 'Whatever Dom has said you've obviously got the wrong end of this. I want *you*, for yourself, for the sweet young person that you are. I've been alone too long, but there was no one to take Elizabeth's place, I admit that. Now there is. But I don't want you to do anything *you* don't want to do. If Dominic mentioned my idea for the remake of "Avenida" it's only because it is the most natural thing to spring to our minds. We're film people, Debra, and that means box-office. And as Elizabeth's daughter, you would be a sensation, I'm not denying that. But if you don't want to try films then you don't have to. Do anything, anything you like, so long as you agree to come back to California with me and let me take care of you.'

'You still want to do that?' she asked disbelievingly. 'After ... after everything that happened this afternoon? I suppose Dominic told you what was said.' Her cheeks burned suddenly.

'Everything. And before we say anything more I'd like to say something in Elizabeth's defence. Earlier, when we talked of Elizabeth and I told you the circumstances of our marriage, I am afraid I may have turned you against your mother quite unconsciously You see, Debra, I did know she didn't love me, and when I said I couldn't forgive her for having you without telling me, that was when I thought ... hoped ... that you might be my daughter.' He shrugged his shoulders. 'That you are not restores some of my faith in my late wife. It seems obvious that she wanted to bring you back to the States, and I'm sure had she done so she would have revealed the facts. She was sometimes impulsive and foolish, but always she inspired love, and not hatred, in her associates.' He looked at her solemnly. 'No matter what your aunt has to say about this I will swear that Elizabeth was not the avaricious creature she made her out to be. Nor did she go around stealing other women's husbands. On the contrary, like Dominic has told you, I'm sure, she was a generous person, and quite incapable of destroying someone's happiness without thought.'

Debra swallowed hard. 'But she did ... steal my aunt's husband.'

'Did she? Or did he perhaps steal her? There are always two sides to every argument. No one will ever know for sure, but it seems obvious to me that your father loved your mother, and as the result of that union you are that most envied of children, a love-child.'

'Envied? I can't believe that.'

'No. Perhaps that was the wrong expression. But, darling, don't become bitter like your aunt. You've your whole life ahead of you. I'm offering you the chance to be free, to be yourself. Why can't you accept it?'

'I couldn't allow you to support me,' she said stiffly.

'But your mother was worth a small fortune——'

'I don't want that money!' Debra bit her lip. 'I ... I couldn't accept it. Not now, anyway.'

Aaron shook his head exasperatedly. 'All right, then. Do as I ask and make a film, the remake of "Avenida" in fact. I'll audition you and train you myself, just as I did Elizabeth. That way you'll be completely independent, and you'll earn enough to live in comfort.'

Debra frowned. 'I wouldn't get a part like that without you, you know that. It would be like charity.'

'God!' Aaron smacked a hand against his forehead. 'Debra, you are the daughter of my dead wife; at least let me do this for you, for my sake if not for your own. Don't be so damned proud! Let me help you, *please*!'

Debra looked up at him, compressing her trembling lips. 'You're very kind.'

'Me? I'm not kind. I'm a businessman!' Then he smiled. 'Darling, darling daughter of mine, I still think of you as this, even now; do as I ask. Come back to California with me, let me worry about you, just for a little while, eh?'

Debra felt a lump in her throat. 'Oh, Aaron,' she said, 'you make me feel ashamed. I'm so ungrateful, and ungracious. All right. I'll come with you.'

'Thank you, *thank you*.' He snapped his fingers peremptorily. 'This calls for a celebration. Waiter! Some champagne!'

It was only later, when Debra lay sleepless in the comfortable bed at the hotel, that she wondered how much her consent had been motivated by the knowledge that by returning to the States with Aaron she would continue to see Dominic McGill, for no matter how she tried, she could not get him out of her mind.

CHAPTER SIX

DEBRA studied her reflection in the full-length mirror of the fitted wardrobe, turning round critically, trying to decide whether the dress she had chosen was suitable. She sighed, and put up a tentative hand to her hair. The new style with the sides of her hair swept up to the back of her head and secured by a diamanté clasp was somehow sophisticated without actually altering the tender curve of her chin and neckline, while her eyes had been expertly made up by Estelle, who Aaron insisted was to be her own personal maid. Her dress was a matt shade of emerald velvet, low-necked, yet with long sleeves ending in a pointed cuff. The short skirt ended several inches above her knees, revealing the slender shape of her slim legs. She knew she had never worn such an expensive dress, yet she was still nervous, and she knew it was all because tonight they were dining at the home of Dominic McGill.

She turned abruptly away from the mirror, and crossing the wide room she helped herself to a long American cigarette from the box on a nearby table. She lit the cigarette with the heavy table lighter close by, then drawing deeply on it she walked to the open french doors which led on to a balcony overlooking the sweep of lawns and landscaped gardens at the side of the huge house. She took a deep breath and tried to calm her shaken emotions.

It was six weeks since she had returned to the States with Aaron. They had returned alone, Dominic McGill and Victor Ross having already left for home. Debra had not seen Dominic alone since the night in the hotel in London, and whenever she had seen him he had been polite and detached, but nothing more.

She bent her head impatiently, glancing at her watch, and then turning back to look at her room. Aaron's home in Los Angeles was the most beautiful place Debra had ever seen, let alone lived in. Its rooms were wide and expansive, with polished floors and thick rugs, deep leather and skin-upholstered chairs and couches, and highly polished darkwood furniture that blended in with the plain washed walls, bright with wall plaques and paintings, And it all had a kind of homeliness, a lived-in atmosphere, which had been lacking in some of the homes Debra had visited since her return to California with Aaron.

They had been invited everywhere, and the press had made the most of the story, when Aaron had been obliged to tell it. Naturally he kept the personal details private, and to all intents and purposes she was his daughter. Whether the press, and the public, believed the story was another matter, but Debra was sufficiently like Elizabeth Steel to cause a minor sensation in her own right.

At first Debra had been overawed and bewildered by the strange and wonderful things that were happening to her. Aaron had insisted that he be allowed to provide her with a wardrobe fitting to her position as his daughter, and although Debra's innate sense of independence had rebelled against such an overbearing attitude her natural womanly instincts had overcome her doubts. It was so nice not to have to think any more, but merely allow Aaron to do all her thinking for her. It was amazing, she thought, how in a comparatively short space of time one could accept a complete change in one's set of values, and adapt accordingly.

She had got to know Aaron's closest friends and

their wives, and had been accepted into their charmed circle. She used the phone regularly, and was now able to talk the small talk so widely used at parties here. She could smile, and act as hostess, and even flirt a little.

Only Dominic McGill caused her any anxiety, and when he was around all her new-found sophistication left her. She didn't understand fully why he disturbed her so, but as she had heard the other women talking about him quite freely, and about how attractive he was, she had begun to believe she was just like them, and she felt a sense of annoyance that she should be so stupid.

In consequence, she was relieved when two weeks after her arrival in the States he had left with a film crew to write the outside shots of a movie being made in South America. Aaron missed him, it was obvious he considered the younger man a very close friend, and it was inevitable that on his return, when he gave a dinner party, Aaron should be one of the guests.

She looked again at her watch. It was a little after eight. Aaron would be waiting for her. She stubbed out her cigarette and left the bedroom reluctantly. As she descended the wide panelled staircase, Aaron came into the hall below and looked up at her.

'Darling,' he exclaimed, 'you look wonderful! I haven't seen that dress before, have I?'

Debra smiled and shook her head. 'No, but I gather you like it.'

'Like it? It's superb. You should wear more velvet, it suits the mattness of your skin. Perhaps a black velvet would be quite striking.'

Debra shook her head as she reached the bottom of the stairs and slid her hand through his arm. 'Aaron, you've spent quite enough money on me already. And I feel such a fraud. I do nothing all day but lie around the house, and then when you come home in the evenings you ask if I'm tired.'

Aaron gripped her hand tightly. 'You're not bored?' he asked, quickly.

'Bored? With that magnificent library at my disposal; with that marvellous collection of records and a stereo record-player; with a car of my own to drive and plenty of friends calling in, or telephoning me? Of course I'm not bored.'

Aaron sighed. 'I sometimes wonder. Debra darling, please don't be afraid to tell me if you're unhappy. I want you to be so happy here that you'll never want to leave.'

Debra smiled, 'I'm happy. But I still feel a fraud. I ought to be doing something.'

'Have you looked at the script I brought you?'

Debra slid away from him. 'Y . . . e . . . s.'

'And?'

'Oh, I've read it all. And the part—even I can see the part of Laura is a marvellous part for any actress, but not *me*!'

'Why not?'

She shrugged. 'I'd make a mess of it.'

'At least try. For me.'

Debra smiled, running her tongue over her pink lips. 'That's blackmail, Aaron.'

'Well, what if it is? Will you do it?'

She shrugged. 'I can't refuse, if it's what you really want. But remember, Aaron, please, I'm not a child. If I'm bad, tell me. Don't let me go on making a fool of myself.'

'All right, it's a deal. This is marvellous! We shall really have some welcoming news for Dominic, shan't we?'

'Dominic?'

'Of course. You knew it was his play.'

'Yes.'

'Well, naturally he takes quite an enormous part in the casting of the film, and if any re-writing needs to be done, he does it.'

Debra flushed. 'Oh, I see.'

Aaron frowned suddenly. 'Say, Debra, what is this? I've noticed lately that whenever I mention Dom's name you clam up. Have you and he had a row or something?'

'Heavens, *no*!' Debra lifted the velvet cape from the heavy chest standing in the hall. 'Darling, it's getting late. We ought to be going.'

'Oh, all right,' Aaron nodded, but his eyes were thoughtful.

Dominic's house in Santa Monica backed on to a stretch of beach bordering the Pacific Ocean. On the way Aaron told her a little about its situation.

'It has its own stretch of beach,' he said. 'And the beaches bordering the Santa Monica Bay are really something! There's surfing, too, if you've ever tried it.'

Debra shook her head and shivered. 'No, I don't surf.'

'Never mind, you'll soon learn. Dom gives surfing parties sometimes, but of course I'm not invited to them.' He grinned. 'I'm a bit long in the tooth for that kind of thing.'

Dominic's house was all white, standing in its own grounds, and surrounded by a high wall. The gate was locked and guarded by a man in uniform controlling a huge white Alsatian. After they had identified themselves, they were allowed to drive up the long curving road which led to the gravelled forecourt of the building, and here they were greeted by a uniformed commissionaire.

'Heavens, is this necessary?' exclaimed Debra, sliding out of the car. 'I mean, you don't have all this security, Aaron.'

Aaron tucked her arm through his. 'No,' he agreed, smiling. 'But then I'm not continually being hounded by the press, and nor do I have the kind of face that appeals to impressionable females. Besides, Dominic has a priceless collection of antique silver and jade. He needs a burglar-proof system for that alone.'

'Oh!' Debra compressed her lips, and tried to still the heavy pounding of her heart. It was infuriating to know that one man could disturb her just by hearing his name.

They entered an arched courtyard, into an inner patio which had a sparkling fountain in its centre. The lighting from hidden bulbs gave the place a fairy-like appearance, while the house which abounded this central courtyard had a low cloistered walk running round it on which thronged many of the guests. Debra estimated that there must have been at least seventy people there already, and that the place was not already crowded was an indication of its size and scope. The courtyard was tiled with mosaic squares, but the house was stone built with marble pillared balconies to all the upper rooms. The colours of the women's dresses were many and varied, and combined to add brilliance to the sometimes shadowed corners. If Debra had thought Aaron's house was impressive, it was because she had not seen Dominic's yet. Already she knew it was the most attractive and individual design she had ever seen, and the huge rooms whose french doors were open to the night air invited further excited inspection. She sighed. She ought to have known that anything Dominic McGill possessed would be unique in every way.

Aaron greeted various people, introduced Debra to friends she had not yet met, and then their host came strolling across to join them. Dressed tonight in a dark dinner jacket, his weeks spent in the hot Brazilian sun adding a fresh and healthy tan to his already dark-skinned features, and his silvery hair bleached a shade lighter, he looked, to Debra, like a lean, sleek tiger, only his blue eyes providing the contrast from the tawny eyes of a jungle beast. She felt a suffocating sense of inadequacy. What woman could possibly interest him enough for him to sacrifice his freedom for her? None that Debra could think of, unless the sultry Marsha Mathews could tame the primitive instincts he possessed. He smiled warmly at Aaron, shaking his hand before he even looked in Debra's direction. Then he did look her way, and his blue eyes were cool and narrowed, the dark lashes veiling his expression.

'Hello, Debra,' he said smoothly. 'How are you?'

'Fine, thanks. How about you?' she answered perfunctorily.

'No complaints,' he replied, glancing round as though bored by this confrontation. Then he looked at Aaron again. 'See me later,' he said. 'I've got all the information we need for "Steps".'

'Good, good.' Aaron nodded, but his eyes were troubled as he surveyed the two of them. 'When do we eat?'

'Any time you like. There's a buffet laid out in the green lounge. Just help yourselves.' The sound of music throbbing came from a room further round the courtyard. 'There's dancing in the ballroom,' he went on. 'I'll see you there later, right?'

'Right,' Aaron nodded, and they watched him walk away towards another group of guests who had just arrived. Then Aaron looked down at Debra. 'Come on, honey. We'll go find where you can hang your wrap, then we'll help ourselves to some drinks—and some food!'

Victor Ross joined them in the lounge as they were eating canapés and drinking champagne. He grinned at Debra warmly and said:

'Hi, Dom told me I'd probably find you here.' He looked at Aaron. 'Would you mind if I stole your partner for a while?'

Aaron looked more relaxed. 'Of course not, Vic. Where are you taking her?'

'To dance, of course. That okay, Debra?'

Debra hesitated. She had no particular desire to go with Victor, when it seemed that Dominic McGill had placed him as her escort. But Aaron was looking at her so intently that she decided she would go as it seemed that was what Aaron wanted her to do.

Victor took her hand, and they walked along the outside walk towards the ballroom. He surprised her by saying: 'You're thinking that I only came because Dom asked me to, aren't you?'

Debra shrugged, 'Well, you did, didn't you?'

'No. *I* asked Dom where you were. I saw you arrive, but then you disappeared before I had a chance to speak to you. And that's the truth.'

Debra smiled a little more warmly. 'I'm sorry, Victor. It's just that I don't want to be anyone's burden.'

'That's the second time you've said that to me,' said Victor, squeezing her fingers. 'Don't say it again. I like you, very much, and I like your company. And not because you're Elizabeth Steel's daughter.'

Debra lifted her shoulders helplessly. 'I guess I'm getting pretty touchy about that.'

'Yes, so stop it! People like you for yourself. Now come on. Can you do that step?'

Debra laughed a little, feeling her spirits lift. 'I think so.'

It was fun with Victor after all. He made no demands on her, and for a while she was able to put

Dominic McGill out of her thoughts. It was only when she was sitting on a low basket couch, waiting for Victor to get them both a drink, that she gave any thought to her surroundings, and realised anew to whom it all belonged.

The ballroom was huge, hung with crystal chandeliers, and lit by clusters of electric bulbs, looking like enormous flowers. The walls were mirror-hung, and ornately worked with gold and silver filigree. The floor was well sprung, and highly polished. When Victor returned with a tall glass of vodka and lime juice for her and rum and coke for himself, he said:

'You wouldn't think there was a swimming pool below here, would you?'

'A pool?' she echoed in surprise.

'Sure. Dom has this indoor pool downstairs, in a sort of hollowed-out cavern, and sometimes he gives parties down there. It's overhung with creepers and palms, and it's quite something, believe me.'

'Oh, I do,' she said, looking down at her drink.

'Yeah. But tonight he's on his best behaviour. Some of his guests are pretty important, or maybe you didn't know.' As she shook her head, he went on: 'Well, there's Senator William Mannering. He's in line for the governorship of this state, and then there's Laurence Golphonse. He's a pretty important guy in the television world. There were rumours last year that he had something to do with the brotherhood, but I guess that came to nothing.'

'The *brotherhood*?'

'Yeah, you know. The Mafia.'

'The Mafia?' Debra's eyes were wide.

Victor chuckled at her expression. 'To go on, there's Dolores Rio Alto, George Vansing, Susan Dennis, Jim Jason; dozens of them. I guess you've heard of them.'

As all the names he had just mentioned were quite

famous film stars, Debra nodded, and he went on, reeling off the names like the credits for some fabulous epic.

'Does ... does Dominic know all these people?'

'Of course. Hell, you don't get to his position without getting to know practically everybody of importance, or of some use to you.'

Debra sighed. 'He's been very lucky,' she said dryly. 'After all, you said youself, you both came from—well —poor families.'

Victor swallowed half of his drink. 'Yes, that's for sure.' His eyes surveyed her thoroughly. 'You're very curious about Dom's background, aren't you? Why?'

Debra turned bright red. 'I don't know why you should imagine that,' she said shortly. 'I was merely making conversation, that's all.'

'Oh, don't be so huffy,' he said, grinning. 'Anyway, you're no different from a million other women I know.'

'If you mean by that that I worship at his throne, then you're very much mistaken,' she said angrily, and then went cold as a shadow fell across them, and she looked up into Dominic's face.

Dominic was not alone. A young girl was with him, no more than Debra's age. She was small and curvaceous, with red-gold hair that was cut close to her head and curled riotously. She was wearing a red dress which should have fought wildly with the colour of her hair, but somehow didn't. She was clinging to Dominic closely, forcing his awareness of her all the time. Debra felt nauseated and refused to look up, sipping her drink, her eyes downcast. After that first devastating look at Dominic's expression she had bent her head.

Victor stood up, at his ease. 'Hi, Dom,' he said. 'Hi, Teresa!'

'Hello, Vicky darling,' the girl's voice was childlike and simpering. 'Long time no see!'

Debra compressed her lips, wishing herself far away. She stood down her drink, and lifted her handbag preparatory to getting a cigarette, but before she could open it, a platinum case was offered to her, and she was forced to look up while Dominic lit her cigarette.

'Thank you,' she said, and half turning in her seat away from the other three, she surveyed the rest of the dance floor. As she moved the swathe of dark hair swung against her cheek, and then sprang back into position.

She did not listen to what the others were saying. She knew she was being terribly rude, but she couldn't help herself. He shouldn't have come over like that, bringing that *girlish* creature with him. She refused to analyse why his actions should disturb her so. She only knew that every time she closed her eyes she could see him, silvery-haired, and yet so tanned and dark-skinned, not fair and freckly as so often went with blond hair; blue-eyed, with those long black lashes, and lean-hipped and muscular.

Then Dominic spoke to her, and she looked round to find he was alone. Victor had taken Teresa to dance. 'Do you want to dance?' he was asking, politely.

Debra moved her shoulders awkwardly. 'No, thank you.'

'Why?'

'Because I don't want to dance,' she replied off-handedly.

'Stop behaving like an idiot,' he exclaimed impatiently. 'Look, there are people watching us with some interest, for God's sake let's dance and be done with it.'

'I didn't ask you to speak to me,' she replied coldly.

His fingers closed round her wrist, and he pulled her

to her feet abruptly, taking her off guard, and the pressure of his fingers hurting her flesh.

'What do you think you're doing?' she exclaimed, in amazement.

'Having you dance with me,' he replied coolly. 'Are you going to struggle and make a scene, because if so I should warn you you're going to look rather ridiculous!'

'How dare you?' she cried, but he ignored her, merely drawing her out on to the dance floor, and putting his arm around her.

The dance was a slow-moving beat number to which most of the couples were dancing together, not at all like the other time they had danced. She was close against the hard length of his body, and wholly and disturbingly aware of him. His right arm was right around her, holding her firmly against him, while he merely held her other hand close against her thigh. His cheek was against her hair, and they moved slowly and languorously around the floor.

'Now this isn't so bad, is it?' he murmured in her ear.

Debra shook her head silently, her fingers on his shoulder appreciating the expensive texture of the material of his suit. A group of three dark-skinned girls had joined the band on their dais and were now singing harmoniously to a popular tune of the day. Debra felt her senses swimming dangerously. The music, the dimmed lights, the blending of exclusive perfumes, and most of all the warmth of Dominic's body were doing crazy things to her metabolism.

Almost without voluntary thought, she slid her arm further round his neck, her slim fingers curving round strands of his hair where it grew down to his collar-line. His hair was thick and smooth, and she wanted to rumple it wildly and have him kiss her and go on kissing her until she was breathless.

The pulsating compulsion of her thoughts seemed to communicate themselves to him, for he drew back, looking down at her with those intensely blue eyes.

'What are you trying to do?' he murmured a little thickly.

'I—I don't know what you mean.' She withdrew her hand abruptly.

'Sure you do. Baby, don't play games with me.'

'I'm not a baby,' she said breathlessly.

'Are you sure?'

'Of course I'm sure.' She looked down at the buttons of his jacket. 'Don't try to embarrass me like this. I'm sorry I was rude to you in the hotel in London. It was unforgivable, what I said. Actually, I ... I wanted to thank you for ... for being there.' Her eyes were troubled when she looked up. 'Don't ... don't be like this, *please.*'

Dominic's eyes had softened miraculously, and her heart turned completely over. 'Come on,' he said, 'let's get a drink. I could use one.'

Debra nodded, and keeping hold of her hand he led her though the crowds to the edge of the dance floor. Immediately a familiar figure grabbed his arm possessively.

'Dom! Where have you been?' It was Marsha Mathews looking exotic in a full-length Indian sari, made of some material that was striped in every colour imaginable. Debra would have drawn back, but he kept a firm grip on her hand.

'Oh, hi, Marsha,' he said casually. 'Enjoying yourself?'

'No. Dom, where are you going?'

'For a drink,' he replied coolly. 'You know Debra Warren, don't you?'

Marsha's cold eyes surveyed Debra sulkily. 'Yes, of

course. So you're Elizabeth Steel's daughter. How *interesting*!'

Debra flushed, and then Dominic was excusing them, and dragging her after him out of the ballroom. She had to run to keep up with him, but after a while he slowed and entering the house through french doors he led the way through a small comfortable dining room to a long hall that stretched as far into the distance as Debra could see. Then it curved round a corner and she realised it must be the central hall of the house. It really was a massive place, and she wondered how anyone could live alone in such an enormous building.

Dominic steered her into a small library and closed the door, leaning back against it with a sigh of relief. 'Lord!' he said. 'Imagine not being able to find peace in your own house!'

Debra smiled, and subsided on to a deep armchair with an extraordinary design which was nevertheless very comfortable. Dominic straightened and walked across to a side table on which was a tray of bottles and glasses. He poured himself a bourbon on the rocks, then handed Debra a glass of some sparkling liquid she didn't recognise.

'What is it?' she asked cautiously.

'A champagne cocktail,' he replied, smiling that lazy smile that had no mockery behind it.

He put a record on the turntable in the corner, and a few moments later a low throbbing rhythm filled the room. Debra frowned, and he said: 'Dave Brubeck.'

She nodded, and relaxed. It was very pleasant here. The walls of the room were lined with books, while on a desk to one side stood a typewriter and several telephones.

'Is this where you work?' she asked.

'One of the places,' he agreed. 'It's where I work if I

want to do my own typing. Usually I dictate and Vic does most of the graft.'

'Oh, yes, Vic,' she smiled. 'He's nice. I like him.'

'Do you?' Dominic swallowed half his drink abruptly. 'Do you find him easy to get along with, is that it?'

Debra shrugged. 'I suppose so.' She bent her head. 'I suppose it's because he's more the kind of person I'm used to. I mean, he has to work for his living——'

'Don't you think I work for mine?' he exclaimed impatiently.

'No. Not in the same way as Victor does. I mean, as you've just said, Victor does all the actual labouring attached to writing. You just have the ideas.'

'*Just*,' agreed Dominic dryly. 'And what about you now? Are you going to try "Avenida"?'

Debra shrugged nervously. 'Aaron wants me to. I don't know. I'll have to try, but I'm sure I'll make one hell of a mess of it.'

Dominic frowned. 'I don't see why you should. Elizabeth took some time before the actual takes were satisfying. The part grows on you. You'll see.' He finished his drink.

Debra studied him thoughtfully while he was pouring himself another drink. 'Was ... was "Avenida" your first play?'

Dominic offered her a cigarette before replying, and after they were both lit, he said: 'Yes. At least, it was the first I thought suitable for production.' He smiled wryly. 'I wrote some pretty torrid stuff in the old days.'

Debra drew on her cigarette. 'You were ... lucky to have the play accepted, weren't you?' she probed gently.

Dominic lifted his shoulders indolently. 'I wouldn't exactly call it luck.'

'What would you call it?'

He smiled a little mockingly. 'What a curious creature you are, Debra. What is it you want to know? About the play? Or about how well I knew your mother?'

'Aaron has talked to me a lot about my mother,' she said, flushing. 'Naturally I'm interested in people who knew her.'

Dominic smiled rather derogatorily. 'Is that so?' he remarked. 'Okay, what do you want to know?'

Debra felt terrible. 'Oh, nothing in particular,' she tried to act carelessly. 'You—er—you knew her quite well, didn't you?'

'I'll go along with that,' he said, nodding.

'Well—oh, heavens, how long did you know her?'

'Approximately six—maybe seven years.'

'Was she—was she very beautiful?'

'Yes.' He was non-committal.

'Am I really very much like her?'

He shrugged. 'In looks you are. Quite startlingly like her. But in every other way, not particularly. You see, I guess she led a different kind of life from the one you've led, and what with coming to the States, and becoming part of the film rat-race, she was much more —how shall I put it?—much more brittle than you are.'

'Harder, you mean.'

'Yes, I guess you could use that word, although I wouldn't. Even though she knew all about life, and various other matters pertaining to it——'

'Sex,' said Debra blankly.

'—okay, sex, she still was a romantic at heart, and she could still be hurt, unfortunately.'

'Unfortunately,' Debra seized on the word.

'Yes.' He swallowed the remainder of his drink. 'Hell, Debra, what do you want me to say? The woman's dead!'

Debra sipped her cocktail speculatively. 'You don't exactly illustrate your statements, do you?' she said. 'I mean, you always act as though I was a little girl who didn't have to be told that Santa Claus was only a figment of her imagination.'

Dominic stared across at her, his blue eyes piercingly cold. 'And you act all the time as though there's some terrible skeleton hiding in my cupboard which I'm afraid to reveal!'

Debra got up, standing her drink down unsteadily. 'Oh, it's always like this,' she exclaimed. 'Why do you have to speak to me so savagely?'

Dominic shook his head, walking slowly across to her. 'Maybe because you make me feel savage,' he muttered. 'You're such an innocent in some ways, and yet you're trying to understand something that ... oh, God!' He sighed, unbuttoning his jacket and running his hand over the close-cut silvery hair on top of his head. He was close to her again, and she felt that terrible sense of inadequacy assail her.

'I—I do know about the birds and the bees,' she said lightly, trying to shed the longing he aroused in her.

He stopped in front of her, looking down at her. 'Do you? That's interesting!' But he didn't sound interested. Debra thought he sounded bored.

Then he put up a hand and unfastened the diamanté clasp from her hair, allowing it to fall forward, framing her face like a black silk veil. He lifted a handful of her hair almost compulsively, caressing it with his fingers. Debra shivered and looked up at him. His face was close to hers, his mouth hard and yet sensual. The music on the turntable swelled to a throbbing crescendo, and with a groan he gathered the handful of her hair tightly, pulling her close against him, his mouth parting her lips, destroying all her preconceived ideas of what a kiss could be like. There was no gentleness in his touch, he held her as though he couldn't stop himself, and his mouth seemed to draw the strength from her body. Her arms slid round him, beneath his jacket, only the thin material of his shirt separating her from the lithe smoothness of his flesh. He kissed her eyes, her ears, her neck and throat, and then sought her mouth again, until Debra thought her body was burning up.

His hands slid down her back caressingly, arousing sensations she had never suspected existed. Only once before had any man kissed her, and that had been back in her student days when a fellow student had dated her a couple of times, and got around to kissing her on their second date. But he had been young and clumsy and inexperienced, while Dominic McGill was an expert, playing on her emotions deliberately, rousing her so that she had no resistance against him.

Then suddenly there was a brief knock at the library door, and with only the faintest hesitation it opened and Aaron Johannson took a step into the room.

'Hi there, Dom, I saw you were——' He halted abruptly, his eyes on Debra. 'Oh! I'm sorry!'

Dominic released Debra slowly and reluctantly, and she put up nervous hands to her hair, trying to smooth it into some semblance of order. Dominic fastened his jacket, gave Aaron a rather wry glance, and then said:

'Don't panic, Aaron. There's no harm done.' He looked back at Debra. 'In any way!'

Debra looked across at Aaron, seeing the genuine bewilderment on his face, and gathering together all her small store of confidence, she walked across to him, sliding her arm through his and saying:

'Did you wonder where I was?'

Aaron shook his head, trying to regain his composure. 'No, not actually. I thought you were with Vic.'

Dominic walked across to the drinks. 'I could use something,' he remarked dryly. 'How about you, Aaron?' He half-smiled sardonically. 'I guess you need one more than I do.'

Aaron nodded, and looked at Debra strangely. 'I—I was coming to find you, Dom. Like you said. About the shots you got in South America. I guess I never thought....' His voice trailed away.

'Forget it,' remarked Dominic, and Debra felt a hot flush sliding up her cheeks at his words. She, too, was recovering from the shock of Aaron's entrance, and by so doing was recalling the abandoned way she had allowed herself to behave. What thoughts were going round in his head now that he should speak of what had just occurred with such derision in his voice? Was he thinking she was just another woman to make a fool of herself over him? Was it that easy for him? She slid her arm out of Aaron's, feeling sick inside. She wanted to get away quite badly now. In these last few moments she had realised that the thing she had most been afraid of had happened; she was *in love* with him! In love with a man who cared no more for her than he did for any of the women who hung around him. Would she become one of them? Hanging on his every word, begging for his attention? *No!*

'I—I think I'll go and find Victor,' she managed to say quite lightly, holding on to the crystal door handle for support.

Dominic looked across at her. 'That's not necessary. What I have to say to Aaron won't take long.' His expression was enigmatic.

She shook her head, moving a step backwards almost defensively.

'No, maybe not,' she said unsteadily. 'But I'm going,

just the same,' and she fled out of the room, closing the door behind her before he could say anything more.

Debra kept out of Dominic's way until it was time for them to go home. It was not difficult to remain hidden among the other guests, and as, when Dominic reappeared, there were plenty of people wanting to speak to him, he did not come looking for her. Aaron found her about eleven-thirty, and said:

'You look pale, honey. Are you all right?'

Debra shook her head. 'I have a bit of a headache,' she confessed nervously. 'Could ... I mean ... could we go home?'

'Home?' he smiled. 'I like to hear you call my house *home*. Sure we can go home. Where's Dom?'

Debra shrugged. 'I—I haven't seen him. Do we ... do we have to say our goodbyes, or couldn't we just phone him later?'

Aaron studied her thoughtfully. 'Okay, let's go.'

Debra sighed as she slid into the back of the huge limousine. Aaron was always so kind, so understanding. He didn't ask a lot of unnecessary questions.

However, once back in familiar surroundings, even Aaron looked a little curious. Then he said surprisingly: 'Do you want to talk about it?'

Debra lit a cigarette with trembling fingers. 'If you like.'

'It's if *you* like,' he said, stretching out lazily on a low couch, loosening the collar of his shirt. 'Pour me a bourbon, baby, and think about it.'

Debra handed him the drink, then shrugged. 'What's there to say? I guess I behaved foolishly. I expect he considers me another conquest.'

'Who? Dominic? I doubt it. He's not like that.'

'Oh, don't expect me to believe that!' she exclaimed sceptically.

'Why not?'

She spread her hands wide expressively. 'Women positively fall over themselves to attract his attention.'

'So what? He's not to blame for what *women* do.'

'I know, but...!' She drew on her cigarette. 'Well, there's that Marsha Mathews, for instance, and another girl called Teresa. They seem to know him very well.' She walked across the room restlessly. 'You told me yourself he was no celibate!'

'I know. He's not. But don't get the idea he goes around making love to every woman he meets, because it's simply not true. He's known plenty of women, but I wouldn't say many women had known him.'

Debra heaved another sigh. 'What are you trying to tell me?'

'Well, honey, I guess I'm trying to let you down lightly. I don't want you to think Dominic's a sonof-a—well, a swine, then, but on the other hand, I don't want you imagining yourself in love with him.'

Debra's cheeks burned, and she turned away. 'That *would* be ridiculous, wouldn't it?' she said tightly.

'Yes, it would.' Aaron studied her back thoughtfully. 'Look, Debra, I brought you out here to enjoy yourself, not to get entangled with a man who knew women while you were just a schoolgirl playing with your dolls.' He smote a fist into the palm of his hand. 'The devil of it is, you're going to be working with him in a couple of weeks' time, and you'll have to learn to take him as you find him.'

'Working with him?' She swung round. 'But ... I mean ... how?'

'The part, the part of Laura in "Avenida". You haven't forgotten, have you?' He looked anxious, and she felt contrite.

'No. No, of course not.' She managed a half-smile. 'I

132

suppose if he can work with me, I can work with him.'

'And that incident tonight,' murmured Aaron awkwardly. 'Honey, don't let that happen again.'

'I won't—but why?'

Aaron stood up and came across to her, gripping her shoulders firmly. 'Honey, Dominic is a great guy, I'd do anything for him, he knows that, but—oh, hell, how do I say it?—he's not the kind of guy to be satisfied with—just—kissing you!'

Debra bent her head in embarrassment, and Aaron breathed down his nose hard. 'Debra honey, think about it. Just to please me.'

She sighed. 'Oh, Aaron, I will,' she said.

Debra did not see Dominic again for several days, even though he came to Aaron's house while she was in. She deliberately avoided him, staying in her room until he had gone, and then colouring when Aaron challenged her about it.

'You can't behave as if he's committed some crime against you, honey,' he said gently, when she reappeared. 'He didn't mention you this time, but he knew you were around.'

Debra's eyes darkened. 'How?'

'It's pretty obvious when Estelle comes in with coffee and asks whether I think *you* would like some.'

'Oh, lord!' Debra twisted her hands together. 'What did he say?'

'Nothing. Dominic's no fool. He knows perfectly well why you're avoiding him, but I don't know really why you're doing it. You're only making things more difficult for yourself. Sooner or later you've got to face him, and you needn't worry that he will force his attentions upon you. He's never found that necessary before.'

'I know, but—Aaron, what can I say when I meet him? I mean—I can hardly treat him exactly the same as before, can I?'

'Why not?'

Debra stared at him. 'I never thought you'd say that!'

'Why?' Aaron sounded a little impatient. 'Look, Debra, this isn't England, nor is Dominic a small-minded creep.'

Debra felt hurt, and turned away. 'I thought you'd understand,' she said disappointedly.

Aaron came across to her and hugged her gently. 'All right. I do understand, but remember, Dominic is my friend. I know you weren't to blame for what happened between you, but nor was he, wholly. You're a very attractive girl, honey, and these things happen, you know!'

'I *do* know that.'

'Okay. Then let's forget it. And from now on, if Dominic comes here act naturally.'

'All right, Aaron, I'll try.'

'Good girl,' he smiled, and she managed a small smile in return. But later, when she was alone in her room, she wondered with a sense of desperation how she was going to carry on as though nothing had happened. After all, for her the most phenomenal thing *had* happened; she had fallen in love with him. How crazy could anyone be? she thought angrily. Falling in love with a man who obviously had no intention of ever getting married. And if he did, he would probably choose some girl from a terrifically important background with stacks of dollars, and the kind of position in society that went with magnificent houses down at Santa Monica, and fast cars, and aircraft, and priceless collections of silver and antiques.

Her opportunity to find out how controlled she

could be came a few days later when Aaron came home with an invitation for her to attend a beach party at Dominic's home.

'A beach party?' she exclaimed, in astonishment. 'But why me?'

'Look, Victor arranges all these invitations,' replied Aaron, sighing. 'Naturally, your name would be on the list. And unless you want to cause talk and speculation, not only among our friends but also in the press, then I guess you've got to go.'

'I see,' Debra nodded. 'It's pretty frightening, isn't it? Not to be able to do what you like simply because of other people.'

'Well, when you're as famous as Dominic then I guess you can do what you like,' said Aaron, smiling. 'But from your point of view, and as we intend filming "Avenida" quite soon, we can't ignore the power of the press.'

'But I don't really care either,' she said, sighing. 'I don't mind if I'm never famous!'

'Well, I do,' said Aaron firmly. 'And much as I would prefer you to refuse, you really can't.'

'Will you be there?'

'No.'

'What?'

'Honey, I told you once before, I'm too old for that kind of thing.'

Debra heaved a deep breath. 'Oh, well. At least Victor will be there.'

'Yes, he will. If you like, I'll have him come and pick you up.'

'Would you? That would be better. I'd feel more at ease with Victor.'

'Okay. That's settled, then.' Aaron touched her cheek tenderly. 'Just don't get into any awkward situations, because I won't be there to get you out of them.'

Debra smiled rather wryly, then went to arrange with their cook what they would be having for dinner that evening. When she was in bed later she lay awake wondering whether it would be necessary to take her bathing suit to that kind of party. She had a bikini which she had never worn yet, which Aaron had insisted she needed. But as she hadn't told Aaron that she couldn't swim he didn't know why she never used the pool. She had lain beside the pool in a sunsuit, but that was all. In a way she felt ashamed of being unable to swim, but she found it difficult to explain that on the very rare occasions she had been to the swimming baths, she had been afraid to take both feet from the floor of the pool. And there had never been anybody interested enough to teach her. She sighed. Well, she thought, if there were as many people at this party as there were at the last one no one would notice whether she could swim or not.

When she broached the subject of what to wear with Aaron he looked astonished.

'Why, you'll wear your swimsuit, of course,' he said. 'You can wear a beach dress or coat if you like over it, but that's all anyone wears to a party of this kind.'

'Oh, I see.' Debra swallowed hard. 'All right.' She mentally ran an eye along the clothes in her wardrobe. She had a caftan-styled towelling beach robe and she supposed that would be the most suitable thing to wear with the bikini. Also she might conceivably be able to keep the robe on, as the thought of walking about in the minute bikini terrified her.

As she dressed on the evening of the party in the bikini, which was made of stretch nylon towelling in a delicious shade of apricot, she spent a moment studying herself in front of the wardrobe mirror. She knew she had a good figure, and her legs were quite long and shapely. She had left her hair loose, and she shivered a little as she stood there. Imagine, she thought with a kind of suppressed panic, imagine meeting Dominic again for the first time in this kind of outfit! She shook her head. She *must* put him out of her mind. It was no good going to this party, thinking about him. She must make herself completely cool and detached.

When she descended the stairs, the caftan's wide sleeves thrown back to reveal the tanned smoothness of her arms, Aaron looked rather thoughtful.

'Let me see the suit,' he said, and self-consciously Debra removed the robe. Aaron nodded solemnly, then sighed, 'Oh, baby, you're *beautiful!*'

Debra flushed, shaking her head. 'Don't say that.'

'Why? It's true. You are beautiful. But for God's sake, be careful! Promise me.'

'I promise. But it's not necessary,' she said awkwardly. 'I mean, I have absolutely no intention of even being alone with that man, let alone anything else.'

'All right,' Aaron smiled. 'The bikini is fine. You'll enjoy it. The water is great in the bay. I expect they'll be surfing, so take care.'

'Yes—yes, I will.' Debra's stomach turned over. *Surfing!*

Victor arrived a few minutes later in an open tourer Cadillac, all ice blue and chrome, and very comfortable. He was wearing beach shorts and a gaudy shirt, hanging loose and unfastened. He looked tanned and handsome, and Debra relaxed a little. With Victor she felt safe. But even his eyes widened at the sight of her, as she hastily wrapped the folds of the caftan about her.

'Say,' he muttered, 'you look really something, honey. That tan you're getting is great!'

'Thank you.' Debra slid into the car. ''Bye, Aaron.'

'Goodbye, baby. See you later.'

The drive out to Santa Monica was accomplished in

a very short time, or so it seemed to Debra. She was always fascinated by the intricate layout of roads in the clover-like pattern and she watched Victor with interested eyes as he expertly negotiated the intersections.

He glanced her way once and said: 'Honey, take your eyes off me. You're making me nervous!'

Debra laughed. 'I don't believe you. You're much too experienced. It amazes me how anyone learns to drive here. Even I keep to the narrower highways, and I wouldn't dare come on to the freeway.'

It was almost dark by the time they arrived at Dominic's house, but as they drove up the drive they could hear the sounds of music coming from the beach below the house, and floodlights dispersed the shadows. There was the inviting smell of roasting meat from the barbecues, and the sound of laughter and voices floating on the air. She relaxed a little. It was obvious that there was already a lot of people here, and Dominic would have little time to bother about a girl who so obviously was scared stiff of him.

They went down to the beach by way of a flight of stone steps hewn into the cliff-face, and Debra removed her sandals as she stepped on to the soft sand. A faint breeze was blowing off the sea, providing a cooling airstream which was very pleasant because it was a very warm evening. There were people everywhere, all talking and laughing, and some dancing to the record-player, the modern dances losing nothing in the transposition from dance floor to beach. In fact, watching some of the girls do seductively limbo-like movements, Debra thought they seemed lost in the sensation of undulating their bodies.

There was lots of food on low trestles, but steaks were being cooked on barbecues, and whole chickens turned on spits. There was the smell of hamburgers and onions, and frankfurters being slid between crumblingly soft bread rolls. Dozens of waiters moved among the crowds with trays of drinks, while bottles of coke and lemonade were stacked in wooden cases for anyone who was merely thirsty.

Now that she was here, Debra saw that none of the guests seemed to be wearing anything but bathing suits, the heat of the night air making any further attire unnecessary. But still she clung to her caftan, making some excuse about feeling cool to Victor when he would have lifted it from her shoulders.

They were joined by another young couple Victor introduced as Eliza and Ben Shawcross, and they all got drinks and stood on the edge of the group of dancers, sipping their drinks, smoking and talking. Eliza was wearing a black one-piece bathing suit, while Ben wore striped Bermuda shorts. Victor explained that Ben was a technician at the studios, and that Eliza was his wife. Debra liked them, and time passed by smoothly. A little later they danced, and Victor said:

'Aren't you going to take that robe off?' He grinned. 'You're acting as though wearing a swimsuit was something to be ashamed of. Hell, it's all quite respectable. Dom doesn't give the kind of parties where they play strip poker!'

Debra smiled, and laughed a little. 'I'm sorry. It's just that I've never worn a bikini before, and it's years since I've even worn a swimsuit.'

'Is it?' Victor looked surprised. 'We'll be surfing later. Are you going to try?'

'Oh!' Debra was nonplussed, still reluctant to reveal that she couldn't swim. 'I don't know. Will you?' She glanced across at the frothy tide roaring in at the shoreline.

'Sure. We all do. But if you're nervous just stay in

the shallows, it can be dangerous further out.'

'Yes, all right.' Debra lifted her shoulders thoughtfully. 'I suppose Dominic is the world champion, or something,' she remarked sardonically.

Victor roared with laughter. 'You must be joking,' he said, playfully touching the tip of her nose with his finger.

Debra grimaced, then the dance was over and they walked back to the others. 'Where is Dominic?' Ben asked, when they joined them. 'I haven't seen him yet.'

'Nor have we,' said Victor. 'I guess he'll be around somewhere. I saw Lindsay Harrigan a while ago, so I guess he's with him. Harrigan is interested in this new play of Dom's. He wants to produce it for the New York Theatre Company.'

Ben nodded knowledgeably, and Eliza smiled at Debra. 'How are you liking living in Los Angeles?' she asked, in a friendly way.

'I—well, I love it,' replied Debra honestly. 'The people are so warm and friendly, and the climate is marvellous.'

'Yes, it is nice, isn't it?' said Eliza, grinning in a satisfied way. 'I've lived here all my life, but I wouldn't change it. Do you get on well with Aaron? He's a nice man.'

'Oh, yes.' Debra was enthusiastic. 'I love him. He's so kind and sweet and generous, and he's very understanding.'

She almost jumped out of her skin when an arm closed round her shoulders and Dominic said softly in her ear: 'Could this be me you're talking about? If so, it's an improvement on the last time.'

Debra looked sideways into his laughing face, and her heart skipped a beat. His eyes were warm and amused, and held no hint of disparagement. Eliza looked a little surprised at the familiar way Dominic looked at Debra, and said: 'Hello, Dominic. So you are here.'

'Hi, Liz!' Dominic grinned at her, more relaxed than Debra had seen him for a long time, but he didn't release her. Instead he stood talking casually to the others, his arm across her shoulders casually, disturbing her in spite of herself.

He was wearing an open-necked navy blue shirt and navy blue shorts, his legs tanned and muscular. He talked to Ben and Eliza as he talked to everyone else, casually, naturally, with no sense of his own importance. Debra thought that was one of the most attractive things about him. He never talked down to people, and when either Ben or Victor or Eliza were talking to him he listened intently to what they were saying without interruption.

Then he looked down at Debra, and she felt suddenly alone with him, in the midst of all these people. 'Come on,' he said softly. 'I want to talk to you—alone.'

Debra felt mesmerised. 'No,' she said, shaking her head, her breath coming in swift gulps.

'Yes,' he said imperviously, his fingers on her shoulder hurting her suddenly. He smiled at the others, ignoring their speculative gazes. As he compelled her to walk across the sand, she wriggled angrily, and he said: 'For God's sake, Debra! What do you expect me to do to you? I won't even touch you if that's more to your liking!' His hand dropped from her shoulder, and she shivered.

'Why do you want to talk to me?' The words were wrung from her.

'You know why. I guess I want to apologise.'

'That's not necessary.'

'I know it's not. But nevertheless I do.' He thrust his hands into the pockets of his shorts. 'Is that why you've been avoiding me?'

Debra shrugged. 'Maybe.'

'You mean *yes*. Okay, now I've apologised, don't go cold on me again!'

Debra felt furiously angry. He was so unaware of the way he could wreak havoc with her emotions. Or maybe he did know. Maybe it amused him a little to see the reaction he had on her.

'I wish you would leave me alone,' she exclaimed icily. 'I was quite happy to stay with Victor and his friends.' She spread wide her hands. 'I don't know why you had to invite me here. All this—doesn't impress me!'

'Why, you——' He bit off an angry epithet. Then he breathed deeply, controlling his temper. 'All right, Debra. Play it your way.' He stopped suddenly and turned back, and she was left to herself entirely.

Conversely, as soon as she was alone she began to wish she had not behaved so childishly and rudely. But unless she allowed a situation to develop that could only end in disaster there was no other way to act. Their physical attraction to each other was real enough, even she knew that, and Dominic was a man used to getting any woman he wanted. But not *me*, she thought, desperately, I won't let it happen!

She rejoined Victor who was now the centre of a crowd of young people. There was much argument and good-natured teasing going on about various people's swimming abilities, and Debra tried to look part of it all, whereas inside she felt she was being torn apart. There was eventually a general move towards the water, and Debra was forced to shed the caftan at last. Relieved to find that no one seemed to consider her in any way out of the ordinary, she allowed herself to be propelled into the water, splashing about in the shallows with as much confidence as she could muster.

Victor was by her side, and he said: 'Come on, I'll race you a hundred yards out and back again.'

Debra was about to confess her inability to swim when Ben joined them carrying a surfboard. 'Say, Vic,' he said, 'there'll be plenty of time for petting later.' He grinned amiably at Debra. 'Okay, we can see she's a doll, but this is a party, not a tête-à-tête!'

Victor laughed. 'You're only jealous, man. But okay, come on, Debra, let's get a board!'

Debra allowed him to precede her up the beach and wondered whether it was possible to use a surfboard without being able to swim. Surely, if she lay on it as she had seen some of the girls doing, and merely paddled it out and then allowed the tide to bring her back, it would be safe enough. She knew it was a crazy idea, but anything was better than telling this crowd of people that she couldn't even *swim*.

She carried her board down to the water, lay on it as she had seen the other girls do and promptly submerged under the waves in the shallows. She came up gasping and spluttering, to find that Victor was already paddling his way out several yards in front of her. He obviously thought she was following him, and she shivered before again trying to mount her surfboard. Once again she received a ducking, and her thick hair was now hanging in black strands about her shoulders. She compressed her lips angrily, then became aware that someone was standing further up on the beach, watching her with mockingly amused eyes.

'What's the matter?' Dominic asked lazily. 'You seem to be having a little difficulty! Or is this a new idea in bathing?' he laughed derisively.

'Oh, you!' Debra turned her back on him and tried again, and again she fell into the water, this time swallowing several mouthfuls so that she felt as though she was choking and she stood coughing ignominiously.

She felt as though she couldn't get her breath, and she left the surfboard, staggering up on to the dry sand feeling nauseated.

Dominic came over and thumped her several times on her back, making her cough even more, but at last dislodging the airlock in her chest. She raised watering eyes to his, and said in a disgruntled voice: 'Thank you.'

'That's okay.' He shrugged and would have turned away, when she said:

'Aren't you swimming?'

'I swim in the pool,' he remarked coolly. 'I never surf.'

'Why?'

'As you're so fond of saying, that is my affair.'

Debra sighed, and wrung out her hair, and Dominic walked away towards the group of people still sitting round the barbecues. Debra stood feeling terribly alone and miserable. Then with another sigh, she walked away along the beach in the opposite direction, away from the floodlights and the music, to where the sand-dunes were moonlit and deserted.

She found a grassy hillock and seated herself upon it, looking back along the shoreline to where the swarms of young people came gliding in on the surf-edged breakers. Some were very good, she had to concede, and she wondered where Victor was, and whether he had missed her yet. There was the comforting sound of their shouts and laughter, and yet she felt totally isolated. Alone with the misery of her thoughts.

She wondered why Dominic didn't surf. It was unusual; he seemed to like most other sports. She wondered how he thought of her. Probably as an over-matured schoolgirl, she thought dejectedly. And yet he found her attractive, and she thought that possibly he was annoyed with himself for feeling so. She returned to the problem of her mother, and wondered again about her relationship with Dominic.

The music on the record-player had changed to a plaintive love song, and Debra felt her heart contract painfully. Was it always going to be like this? Was she always going to have to live with this terrible pain in her inside, every time someone mentioned Dominic's name, or every time she saw him, walking or talking to Aaron, or merely passing by in the Ferrari?

She looked out across the wide expanse of the Pacific Ocean. It was such a peaceful scene, the moon lighting the sky and making silver balls of the fleecy clouds. The midnight blue of the sky was alight with stars, and the horizon was a blending of blue and turquoise. She cupped her face in her hands; she ought to be happy here. She was the luckiest girl in the world. Anyone would be thrilled to change places with her; why then did she feel this compelling urge to run away, to *escape*, if not mentally, then at least physically?

It was then that she saw the dark object being beaten mercilessly by the tireless surf, as it broke in creamy waves on the beach. She stood up, shading her eyes, trying to distinguish what it might be. It was not small; in fact, it looked remarkably like a *body*.

Debra did not stop to think. She ran swiftly down the grassy slope, across the beach to where the waves were shifting the sand. Now that she was closer she could see that it was a body, a girl's body, and with trembling limbs she stepped into the water quickly before she had the chance to think about it.

The waves came roaring in at her, and the girl's hair was spread like seaweed in the gloom. Debra shivered in spite of herself; there was something terrifying about dragging a body out of the sea. How long had it been there? Was it already dead? And if so, for how

145

long?

She was almost breast high in the water when the waves brought the girl's body surging against her. Swallowing her fear, she grabbed at it wildly, almost losing her balance in the process, and letting out a sharp cry. Then, with panting breath, she managed to turn, pulling the body after her. It was too heavy for her to lift out of the water, and she staggered desperately back through the waves to the shallows, dragging the body at last out on to the dry sand of the beach.

Then, shivering, she knelt beside it, turning it over and feeling shakily for the heart. To her relief the girl's features were not distorted, so obviously she had not been in the water long. There was the faintest of heartbeats, but Debra knew that this was almost certainly just a nervous reaction, and that unless immediate resuscitation was given she would die. She looked about her wildly. What did she know of life-saving? Practically nothing. The girl was probably full of water.

With desperate speed, she turned the girl back on to her stomach, forcing her arms behind her, pressing hard on the girl's diaphragm. Water spurted out of the girl's mouth, and Debra repeated the action, closing her eyes and praying she was doing the right thing.

Then she heard voices, and the swish of feet across the sand, and a young man was lifting her to her feet saying: 'We heard you shout. Come on, I'll take over. You look worn out.'

All at once there were dozens of people around. Some were sent running for assistance while others got wraps for the girl, and chattered in excited voices about it. It seemed the girl was from the party, her surfboard had been washed up on the beach, and they had been searching for her since.

Debra stepped back, herself more than a little shaky

now, and wishing she had something to drink to take the chill out of her bones. It was the shock of actually finding a body in the water, dead or alive, that had temporarily robbed her of all strength, and she felt as weak as water. She sank down on to the sand, out of the circle of rescuers, and rested her head on her knees wearily.

Then she heard Dominic's voice, looked up and saw him pushing his way through the crowd surrounding the girl, who now seemed at last to be responding to treatment. He looked distraught, and thrust the others aside carelessly, kneeling down beside the girl on the sand and staring at her with intent eyes. Debra shivered again. Was this yet another of the women who seemed to follow him wherever he went? She bent her head again, and forced the hot tears back.

She was shaken abruptly out of her lethargy, as strong hands wrenched her to her feet, she shook back her damp hair to stare at Dominic uncomprehendingly.

'It *is* you!' he muttered violently. 'Oh, thank God!' He held her face between the palms of his hands. 'Are you all right? Was it you who pulled Annabel out of the water?'

Debra nodded, trembling quite badly now.

'Hell,' he muttered, 'you're freezing! Come on, I'll take you up to the house!'

Without giving her a chance to protest, he swung her up into his arms and strode away along the beach, many eyes turning questioningly in their direction, as the emergency with the half-drowned girl gave way to a more intimate kind of speculation.

Debra didn't particularly care what they thought. She felt too warm and secure in Dominic's arms to care whether she was being talked about. The steep steps up the cliff must have taken all of Dominic's strength,

147

and he walked more slowly across the lawns and into the courtyard of the house. They entered into the wide hallway, and were met by a white-coated servant who looked anxiously at them and said:

'Is this the young lady who was injured, Mr. Dominic?'

'No,' replied Dominic shortly. 'Have you arranged for an ambulance?'

'Yes, sir.'

'Good. I'll leave you to deal with it, then. Ask Joseph to bring some towels and a robe to my study, at once.'

'Yes, sir.'

Dominic stood Debra on her feet in the comfortable surroundings of his study, then flexed his back muscles tiredly. Debra watched him; it was the first time she had seen that taut, withdrawn expression on his face. She half-thought he was in pain, and asked:

'Are ... are you all right?' tentatively.

Dominic nodded his head. 'Are you?'

Debra shrugged. 'Of course,' then another servant arrived with an arm full of towels, and a white bath-robe over his shoulder.

'You wanted these, Mr. Dominic?' he asked, looking curiously at Debra.

'Yes, thank you, Joseph.' Dominic took the things with a brief smile of thanks, then the door closed and they were alone. Immediately Debra was assailed with nervous reaction, but Dominic merely threw a couple of huge bath-towels at her and said, pointing to a door: 'There's a bathroom through there. Go dry yourself, and take off that wet costume or you'll catch a chill.' He handed her the robe. 'Put this on, then come back and have a drink. You look as though you could use one.'

Debra hesitated only momentarily, then walked

through the door, closing it behind her and sliding home the bolt with a definite click. A few minutes later she emerged feeling considerably warmer and dryer, her hair hanging in damp tendrils about her shoulders. She felt awkwardly aware of the unconventionality of her attire, and wished she had thought to bring some clothes with her, just in case she had needed them.

But Dominic was stretched out on a low green velvet-covered couch, his eyes closed until he became aware of her presence. Then he propped himself up on one elbow and nodded across to the drinks cabinet. 'I've poured you a brandy and soda,' he indicated. 'Drink it, it'll restore your moral fibre.'

Debra didn't know whether he was mocking her or not, but she did as he suggested, and stood drinking the fiery liquid and looking at him, wondering why he had not risen at her entrance. It was not like Dominic to lack the simple courtesies.

He lay back on the couch, as though she were not there for a moment, then, with obvious difficulty, he got to his feet. Debra stared at him anxiously.

'There is something wrong,' she said positively. 'What is it?'

'Nothing that need concern you,' he replied briefly. 'Now tell me, what are you trying to do to me?'

Debra stood down her empty glass, sliding the palms of her hands into the sleeves of the robe. 'I don't know what you mean,' she said, shaking her head.

He walked towards her slowly, and looked down at her with a strange expression in his eyes. He lifted a strand of her hair and twined it round his fingers. 'Don't you know that I thought it was you half-drowned in the water?' He tightened his hold on her hair, hurting her momentarily. 'You had disappeared, no one seemed to know where you had gone, and then this guy came rushing along the beach yelling that some girl had been found almost drowned. Hell, what else was I to think?'

Debra bent her head. 'I'm sorry.' She sighed. 'I always seem to be apologising to you.' Then she looked up. 'Is the girl going to be all right?'

'Yes. I guess you practically saved her life. If you hadn't been in that particular area she might easily have been washed out to sea by the tide.' He frowned. 'Anyway, why were you there, out of sight of everyone?'

'Just sitting,' said Debra defensively.

'Alone?'

'Obviously.'

'Yes—obviously,' he echoed, nodding.

Debra pulled her robe closer about her, conscious suddenly of the scarcity of her attire. And Dominic was too close for the normal functions of her body to act normally. Her heart was pounding, and she felt hot all over. Could that be the brandy?

'I'd—I'd better go,' she stammered. 'Victor will be wondering where I am, too.'

'Does that bother you? What Victor thinks?'

Debra stiffened. 'Not particularly, should it?'

'That rather depends,' he murmured, his eyes caressing suddenly.

'Oh, Dominic,' she breathed, aware of the heightened tension. 'Don't *touch* me!'

His fingers fell away from her hair. 'Am I so repulsive to you?'

'You're not—repulsive at all,' she said, looking at him for a moment. '*Please*, get Victor to take me home.'

'All right, all right!' He swung away from her. Then he looked back at her over his shoulder. 'Tell me the truth, Debra, you can't swim, can you?'

She flushed. 'Why ask me that?'

His eyes were hard now. 'Because I had to know that I was right. I had to know that there was some justification for my anxiety about you.' He looked at her with exasperation. 'You have no idea what risks you took, walking out into that ocean! God, if you'd been swept off your feet——'

She shivered. 'But I wasn't!'

'No. But you very easily could have been. Do you think I want the responsibility for your death on my hands?'

'That's a horrible thing to say!' Debra was nearly in tears now. 'I'm sorry if I caused you unnecessary concern. In future I'll try to keep out of your way and then that won't happen.' Her voice broke.

'*Debra!*' he groaned, and turning, he pulled her close to him, his mouth seeking hers. There was a wild pulsating emotion in his kiss that momentarily drove all thoughts of escape out of her mind. Instead she wound her bare arms round his neck, twining her fingers in his hair, and returning his kiss with all the warmth and passion he desired.

At last the kiss ended, and Debra became aware of her situation, the isolated intimacy of the room, the inviting softness of the couch, and the bathrobe which could only be his.

With a stifled exclamation, she dragged herself out of his arms and ran to the door. Wrenching it open, she ran down the hall, almost cannoning into a girl coming from the opposite direction. She apologised automatically, then recognised the cold features of Marsha Mathews. The other girl caught her arm, her narrowed eyes taking in Debra's tousled hair, and hastily tightened bathrobe.

'Have you been with Dom? Where is he?' She almost spat the words.

Debra shook herself free. 'He's—he's in the study.'

'Are you leaving?'

'Yes.' Debra's cheeks burned.

'Good. I guess you finally got the message,' remarked Marsha spitefully. But Debra did not reply. She was already on her way down the hall on trembling legs.

CHAPTER SEVEN

THE following day Debra lived in fear of Dominic arriving unexpectedly at the house. Aaron had to go to the studios and she was left for several hours alone, but he did not come. She did not know whether to be glad or sorry, but knowing Dominic as she was beginning to she doubted whether he would allow things to rest so carelessly. She knew he was attracted to her, but physical attraction did not last, and Dominic seemed to have had plenty of them and Debra determinedly refused to consider herself in such a light.

She spent the day browsing restlessly about the house, unable to settle at anything. She wished desperately that she had never taunted him that evening in the hotel in London, for that was when he began to treat her differently, and it was all her own fault. She had wanted him to notice her, she had been piqued at his apparent lack of interest, at his casual, almost avuncular treatment of herself, and now she found herself in a situation that seemed insoluble.

She glanced at her watch. It was a little after four-thirty, Aaron would be home soon. She lit a cigarette and walked out on to the verandah. The sound of a car's wheels swishing on the drive brought her nervously to her feet, but the car was unknown to her, a blue Cadillac, and it was driven by a woman with a white chiffon scarf protecting her hair.

Debra frowned, and walked to the top of the steps as the car halted at their foot. When she recognised Marsha Mathews she felt an awful sense of foreboding.

Marsha slid out, slamming the car door, and walking up the steps towards Debra with a rather mocking expression on her face. Debra compressed her lips for a moment, and then said: 'Hello, Miss Mathews. Do you want to see Aaron?' She shrugged. 'I'm afraid he's not here yet.'

Marsha studied her insolently. 'No, darling, I don't want to see Aaron. I want to see you.'

'Me?' exclaimed Debra. 'Why? I don't think we have anything to say to one another.'

'Not on the porch we haven't, darling, but if you'll show your innate good manners and invite me in, I think you'll find we have plenty to say to each other,' retorted Marsha.

'I don't think so,' murmured Debra slowly.

'Why? Frightened?'

'What have I got to be frightened of?' asked Debra, stiffening.

'That's for you to decide, darling. Come on, invite me in, there's a good girl. It's hot out here.'

'I'm not your good girl, and stop calling me darling,' said Debra tightly. 'Please go. We have nothing to say to one another.'

Marsha was losing patience. 'What do you want me to say here? A little of what I came about? Then will you invite me in? Okay, honey, how about Dominic McGill's relationship with your mother, for starters?'

Debra's cheeks at first flushed, paled a little. 'What do you know about my mother?'

'Ask me in, and I'll tell you.' Marsha gave a short laugh. 'I'm sure you don't want all the servants to listen to our conversation.'

Debra was breathing swiftly. She glanced about her in a tense, almost frightened way. But her curiosity would not allow her to let Marsha get away with that. For too long these thoughts had plagued her mind.

Marsha saw her indecision, and acted upon it. 'Come on, Debra. You know you want to know the truth, don't you? After all, she was your *mother*, wasn't she?'

Debra turned round abruptly. 'Oh, come in,' she said, pressing the palms of her hands to her cheeks and leading the way into the house.

In the wide lounge, Marsha made herself comfortable on the couch, then said: 'I'd like a Martini cocktail, if that's not too much trouble.'

Debra hesitated, about to deny her anything, but then changing her mind she walked to the cabinet and made the drink with trembling fingers. After Marsha had tasted the cocktail and found it to her liking, she lit a cigarette and said:

'All right, Debra, now we can talk. I thought it was about time someone put you wise to things. I mean, it's pretty obvious that this thing you have for Dom isn't —how shall I put it—serious. I mean, you're attracted to him, but aren't we all, after all, and I don't like to see you being—*used*!'

'Used?' said Debra faintly.

'Yes, darling, *used*! How much do you know about Dom and your mother?'

Debra felt a little nauseated. 'What's there to know?' she countered.

'Plenty,' remarked Marsha sneeringly. 'My dear innocent little Debra, your mother and Dominic McGill were more than just good friends!'

'No!' Debra shivered. 'Why are you saying these things?'

'Because they're true, only no one else would break that glass bubble you're living in and tell you the truth! Good lord, surely you must have guessed he knew her rather well!'

'Of course—they were friends.' Debra felt the words

were stupid and stilted, and did not carry much conviction.

'*Friends!*' scoffed Marsha, a mocking smile on her face. 'Some friends, honey. Ask him how he afforded a trip to the Philippines only a couple of weeks after his first play was read by Aaron Johannson. Ask him that! And see what he says.' She swallowed half her drink. 'Dear Elizabeth took him with her. She needed a rest, or so the doctor was supposed to have recommended. Some rest, with McGill along for the ride!'

'Stop it!' Debra clenched her fists. 'I don't believe you! I—I won't believe you!'

'Why not? Dominic's no saint. He never pretends to be one. And good luck to him! I don't give a damn how many women he's had affairs with. But you, with your silly little ways, imagining that Dominic's interest in you is a personal thing! That's what bugs me! He's using you, honey. You're Elizabeth Steel all over again, and when he holds you in his arms he's thinking of *her*!'

'No!'

Debra turned away. She couldn't bear to listen to any more. It was all that she had feared in her darkest moments, and worse. Dominic had known Elizabeth was married to Aaron, and yet he had cared so little that.... She couldn't think of it any more. It made her feel sick. She swung round on Marsha, who had stood up, and was looking at her with triumphantly amused eyes.

'You see, kid, we had plenty to say to one another.' Marsha stood down her glass. 'I guess that's all, then. I'd better be going. I'd hate to be here when dear old Aaron comes home. He and I just don't get along. G'bye, honey. Think it over. I think you'll find it rings true.'

She sauntered to the door and went out, leaving

Debra to her own misery. Even in the argument with Aunt Julia she had not felt as bereft as she felt now. Then, Dominic had been there, to help and comfort her, but now even his presence was suspect. If what Marsha had said was true he had deliberately misled her, not so much by what he had said but by what he had let her believe. All those things he had told her about her mother, how generous and loving she had been, could all be lies, arrant lies, calculated to exonerate Elizabeth, and himself, from the web of their deceit. Oh, how could he? *How could he?*

She sank down on to the nearby armchair, burying her face in her hands, hot tears sliding down her cheeks. If her situation had seemed impossible before, it was ten times worse now. She could not work with him, knowing how he had treated her, when all the time he had been using her as a substitute for her mother. It was sickening, anyway. If Elizabeth were alive today she would be fifty-four years old, a woman in late middle age, completely unsuited to the kind of existence that McGill led.

She sighed, dried her eyes and made her way slowly up to her bedroom. Her mind was in a turmoil, and she took a couple of aspirins to assuage the throbbing pain in her temples. Aaron would be home soon, and she must not show him that she was disturbed. He was fond of Dominic, he treated him like a valued friend; obviously he was completely unaware of what had been between his wife and the young playwright.

She sat in front of her dressing-table mirror, seeing the dark lines around her eyes, evidence of the previous night's lack of sleep. She needed time to think, time to work out what she could do now. Without hurting Aaron in the process there seemed nothing.

She stood up, lighting another cigarette, and thinking inconsequently that she was smoking far too much.

But lately she seemed to have been living on her nerves, and smoking helped.

By the time Aaron came home at six-thirty, however, she was able to meet him quite calmly, her mind already half made up as to what she must do. She had changed into a slim-fitting black skirt which brushed the floor as she walked, and a white chiffon blouse with ruffles around the neckline. Her hair, loose about her shoulders, looked heavy and smooth as silk, and Aaron smiled at her with great warmth as she kissed his cheek in welcome.

'You look charming,' he murmured. 'Are you going out this evening?'

'No. Have you made any arrangements?'

'Not exactly. Tell me, did you know Dom was ill?'

Debra's heart skipped a beat, but she turned into the lounge casually enough, fingering the polished surface of a lacquered cabinet. 'No. Is he?'

'Yes. At least perhaps *ill* is the wrong term. He's strained the muscles of his back. Apparently he was too energetic last evening, and that old injury is troubling him.'

Debra's fingers stopped their tracery. 'Last evening? But——' she ran a tongue over suddenly dry lips. 'Did you find out why?'

'No, not actually. I guess he surfed after all, despite the fact that he knows he's not supposed to. But knowing Dom, sooner or later he was bound to tire of the restriction.'

Debra seated herself on the couch. 'You mentioned a back injury. What back injury?'

Aaron walked over to the drinks cabinet. 'When he crashed the Porsche, years ago.' He turned holding a glass of bourbon. 'Of course there's no reason why you should have heard of it. But he had a severe back injury. It wasn't at all certain that he would walk at first, but then Dom—I guess he has a marvellous strength of will.' He swallowed the drink.

'But he swims—and dances. Doesn't that bother him?'

'Not particularly. It's only the very strenuous activities he has to beware of. And even then—well, I mean, he has surfed, but he's gotten away with it before.'

Debra swallowed hard. If she told Aaron how Dominic had strained his back she would have to tell him the whole story, and quite frankly she had avoided mentioning anything about the previous evening's party. Victor, when she found him, had brought her home, and Aaron had retired early, alleviating any necessity to make explanations.

'I see,' she said now, bending her head. 'How is he, then?'

'Better in health than temper,' replied Aaron, with a smile. 'He hates any kind of fuss, but in this instance he's completely unable to prevent it. I guess he'll be up and about in a day or two, but until then I pity his poor staff.'

'You've seen him?'

'Sure, he phoned me this morning, and we lunched together. Why? Do you want to see him?'

'*No!*'

Aaron shrugged. 'Okay, okay, don't blow your top! Haven't you gotten over that little bit of bother yet? I thought last night would have made you see how unfounded your attitude was. Anyway, I shall have to go see him tonight. He was due to go to 'Frisco tomorrow. There's a conference there that one of us is bound to attend. I guess that only leaves me.'

Debra looked up. 'You're going to San Francisco?'

'Yes. Why? Want to come and keep me company?'

'No. That is—well, it's not that, Aaron. It's just I'm getting used to this place now, and I don't really want

159

to leave it. Besides, I half-promised I'd lunch with the Blairs tomorrow.'

'That's all right,' Aaron smiled. 'You don't have to make excuses, honey. I know how you feel. There are plenty of young people here for you to run around with. If you go to 'Frisco with me you'll be bored to tears with a lot of old men, isn't that it?'

Debra flushed. 'Aaron, you make me feel terrible!'

'Nonsense. I understand. I'm only glad you're settling down at last. I want you to be so happy here, Debra. You know I'd do anything to ensure your happiness.'

Except the one thing necessary to restore my peace of mind, thought Debra wearily. She felt selfish and deceitful, knowing what thoughts were buzzing round in her head, thoughts that were going to be made facts so much easier because Aaron was going away.

'How—how long do you expect to be away?' she asked casually.

Aaron shrugged. 'Two, maybe three days. Why? Have we any arrangements made?'

Debra lifted her shoulders helplessly. 'I don't think so, Aaron.'

'Good.' He sighed tiredly. 'Now I must go and change before dinner. I feel hot and sticky, and I need a shower.'

Aaron went to change, and Debra walked across to the open french doors and stepped out on to the verandah where earlier she had watched Marsha Mathews arrive. Aaron was going away. She would have forty-eight hours at least in which to carry out her plan.

Aaron left the next morning soon after ten o'clock. After he had gone Debra ran upstairs and pulled out the suitcase which she had packed the previous evening from the wardrobe. In it she had placed all her real belongings, the things she had brought when she first came to the States. She was wearing the orange-tweed suit, which while being overly warm for the hot California climate would be the ideal thing for London.

She had checked with the airport the previous evening and found there was a flight leaving for New York at noon today. She had booked a seat on it, and ordered a cab to pick her up from Aaron's house. She had accomplished all this while Aaron was visiting Dominic McGill, and although her conscience troubled her that she should treat Aaron so shabbily, her lack of mental control was panicking her into thoughtless action.

Downstairs the maid, Estelle, approached her.

'You're going away, Miss Debra?' she asked, with obvious surprise. 'Mr. Johannson didn't say nothing about you going away.'

Debra managed a light smile. 'I—er—I'm just going to stay with friends—overnight, that's all, Estelle. Mr. Johannson probably forgot all about it. His trip was so unexpected, I suppose he had other things on his mind.'

'Y—e—s,' said Estelle slowly, 'I guess that could be so. Where can we get in touch with you, Miss Debra? If we should need you.'

Debra hesitated. 'Why—er—that won't be necessary, Estelle. I'll be back tomorrow night. Long before Mr. Johannson returns.'

Estelle folded her arms a little belligerently. 'Surely you can give us a telephone number, Miss Debra.'

Debra compressed her lips. 'I think you're exceeding your position, Estelle,' she said coldly, hating herself for being so unkind.

Estelle's good-natured face lost its vitality. 'I'm sorry,

miss,' she said stiffly, and turning walked away along the corridor towards the kitchens.

Debra watched her go, sighed, then walked into the lounge to watch for the cab.

It was all remarkably easy, after all. Her flight to New York was uneventful, and once there she was able to transfer to a Boeing which would take her to London. She had made the journey to London so recently, with Aaron and Dominic and the others, that she felt no qualms about arranging her tickets and so on, and knew the way through the customs hall quite faultlessly.

Unfortunately, the huge air-liner developed a slight engine fault and they were forced to land at Gander, and it was delayed by several hours. Debra, seething with impatience to be back on British soil, wondered whether anyone had yet discovered her deception. It was doubtful whether Aaron would be back from San Francisco, and there was no one else likely to question her whereabouts immediately.

At last they were airborne again, and it did not seem long before they were banking preparatory to landing at Heathrow. The ground rushed up to meet them, and Debra heaved a sigh of relief as the undercarriage made contact with the smooth area of the tarmac. She was back in England. Back among the people and places she had known all her life.

When she reached the registration she handed over her passport unthinkingly, her mind jumping ahead to her immediate plans. She would get a room in a small hotel tonight, and tomorrow she would go down to Valleydown and enquire whether her position at the secondary school was still vacant for her. The exchange teacher would be leaving at the end of the summer term, and in September there seemed no reason why she should not recommence her job as though none of the things that had happened to her had occurred. In time she would be able to put them completely out of her mind, and if Aaron came after her she would have to tell him the truth.

The clerk at the desk was speaking to her. 'Miss Warren?'

'Yes.' Debra swung her thoughts back to the present. 'I'm sorry. What were you saying?'

The clerk smiled. 'Would you come this way, Miss Warren? There is some question of your entry into the country.'

'What!' Debra felt a butterfly feeling in her stomach. 'I don't understand.'

'Just come this way, Miss Warren.' The clerk looked apologetic, and the other passengers were eyeing her rather strangely. She felt terrible. She followed the clerk through a door behind the desk, and found herself in a small office. The clerk closed the door and she was alone, or not quite alone. The high-backed swing leather chair behind the desk was turned away from her, and as the clerk closed the door it revolved slowly to face her. Then she gasped: 'You! But—you *can't* be here.'

Dominic smiled sardonically. 'Oh, but I can!'

CHAPTER EIGHT

DEBRA'S legs gave way and she bumped down unceremoniously on the chair opposite Dominic McGill. The blood seemed to have drained out of her body, and she felt weak and helpless, completely incapable of conducting any kind of intelligent conversation with *him*.

'Don't look so shattered,' he said harshly. 'You must have known one of us would come after you. It's only fortunate that I found you had gone when I did, or Aaron might easily have had a nasty shock.'

'I don't understand.'

'Don't you? It's quite simple really. I had foolishly expected you to accompany Aaron when he came to see me the night before he left. As you did not, I rang you the following day. I found you were not available.'

Debra shook her head. 'What made you think I might have come to England?' she asked tiredly.

'Various reasons, the most potent being our last encounter.'

'Why?' The word was wrung from her.

'Because you must have known I wouldn't leave it alone.'

Debra flushed. 'It seems I was right.'

'Damn right,' he muttered angrily, leaning forward in the chair.

'I—I thought you were injured. I mean—your back!'

'My back is immaterial in all this——'

'No, it's not. I understood you were practically paralysed.'

Dominic looked sardonic. 'And how much you

164

cared!' he bit out furiously. 'If you insist on speaking about it, at least don't give me any false sympathy!'

Debra's eyes widened. 'It was a purely impersonal interest,' she managed to retort.

'Obviously. Why do you want to know? So that you can gloat over my indisposition. No, thanks!' He lit a cigarette and drew on it deeply. Then he got to his feet and walked round the desk to her side, causing her nerves to stretch vulnerably. 'So, little Debra, now you can answer a few questions for me. Why did you run away like that? What precipitated your flight? Our—shall we say—contretemps? And just what do you expect to do now that you're here?'

Debra studied the ovals of her nails. 'You're so sarcastic, aren't you?' she said, biting her lips to stop them from trembling. 'You're really enjoying baiting me, aren't you?'

'Not particularly. I would prefer to be in my bed, if you must know,' he returned coldly. 'Despite my obvious capabilities, I still have considerable discomfort, which should please you greatly, and therefore the sooner this interview is terminated and we're both on our way back to L.A. the better I shall like it.'

Debra could not prevent the surge of loving concern he aroused in her, and her heart twisted at the knowledge that this might be the last time she spoke to this man. How could she leave him like this, never to know what became of him? And then she remembered why she was escaping and her determination hardened. Always he had this completely disastrous effect upon her. Right now she longed to throw herself into his arms and forget all that was past in the passionate satisfaction of his lovemaking, uncaring of what eventually would follow.

'I ... I'm not going back,' she said now, with determination in her voice. 'I don't care what you do with the money, or anything. I just want to be left in peace. I'm sorry about Aaron. Naturally I shall write and explain, but it's over. Irrevocably.'

Dominic smote his fist down hard upon the table at her side, causing her to start jerkily. 'You're a selfish, spoilt little brat,' he muttered angrily. 'What the hell do you mean by saying you will write to Aaron and explain? What can you explain? What possible reason can you give for breaking an old man's heart!'

'You're a fine one to talk about breaking hearts,' Debra was stung to retort.

'What does that mean?' His tone was menacing.

'Exactly what you think it means,' she said angrily.

'You have me at a disadvantage,' he said savagely. 'Whose heart am I supposed to have broken? I gather that's what you meant.'

'In a way.'

'Oh, come on, Debra, spit it out. Stop fencing with me, or by heaven, I really will lose my temper!'

Debra stood up herself now. 'All right, Mr. McGill, I'll tell you. My actions were precipitated by something—something more than your—your lovemaking! All right, that is part of it, I don't intend you to treat me as you've treated all those other women, but that wasn't all, not by a long chalk. Think back, Mr. McGill. Ten years back. My mother, in fact.'

Dominic's eyes narrowed. 'Go on.'

'Marsha Mathews came to see me,' cried Debra hotly. 'She told me it was time my eyes were opened to what really happened between you and my mother. She said you were her lover! My mother's *boy-friend*!'

Dominic's hard blue eyes were like ice chips. 'Marsha told you this?'

'Yes. And that's not all. She also made it clear that Elizabeth Steel was responsible for the precipitation of your success!' She turned away unable to look at him any longer. 'It's awful! It's disgusting!'

Dominic was perfectly still for a moment. 'Marsha told you this,' he repeated, and when she nodded, he said: 'And you believed her?'

'Of course I believed her.' Debra pressed the palms of her hands to her burning cheeks.

Dominic said nothing more. He merely walked to the door and went out, closing it quietly behind him, an action controlled and yet savage. Debra stood quite still now, raising her face questioningly. He had *gone*! It could not be possible!

She swung round. The room was empty. She was alone.

A tentative knock heralded the arrival of the desk clerk. 'Everything is settled now,' he said politely. 'If you'll come through I can clear you for entry now.'

Valleydown looked exactly the same as it had done eight weeks previously. Its long main street looked narrow and drab after the brilliant colour and warmth of California. The houses seemed small and confined, and even the secondary school seemed old-fashioned and restrictive. Debra left her luggage at the bus station, then walked through the town to the school. Miss Gantry, the headmistress, welcomed her warmly, taking away a little of the chilled, isolated feeling she had felt when Dominic walked out on her.

'I understand you gave up your position in the United States,' remarked Miss Gantry, looking questioningly at her. 'Something to do with your personal situation, I believe.'

Debra nodded. 'Is it necessary for you to know the details, Miss Gantry?' she asked quietly.

Miss Gantry frowned. 'No, not absolutely, although I must confess that the situation intrigues me. After all, you were so *keen* to go to America. I cannot conceive

167

what could have happened to make you change your mind.'

Debra sighed. 'It's a long story. But just now I don't feel much like talking about it. You see, things didn't work out, and quite honestly my life has seemed to be torn apart.' She looked round her at the familiar study. 'I'm enjoying just coming back here, doing ordinary things again.'

The headmistress gave an understanding smile. 'All right, my dear, I won't tax you with it. But do feel you can confide in me if you find yourself in difficulties.'

'Thank you.' Debra looked down at her hands. 'Do you—I mean, do you happen to know of any suitable lodgings available here in the town?'

'Lodgings? But your aunt——'

'My aunt and I are separated, said Debra shortly. 'But I need somewhere to stay, and I've never been faced with this situation before.'

'I see.' Miss Gantry compressed her lips. 'I believe a Mrs. Harrison, in Queen Street, takes in paying guests. When we had a relief teacher several months back he stayed there. I should try it anyway. If she can't take you she may know of someone who can.'

'Thank you. And my job here? My teaching position?'

Miss Gantry shrugged. 'Naturally the job is still yours,' she replied kindly. 'After all, Miss Phillips will be leaving at the end of the summer term to return to the States. You will be able to carry on as usual after the summer vacation.'

'Oh, thank you, *thank you*!' Debra breathed a sigh of relief.

'Did you think otherwise?'

'Well, after the way I acted in San Francisco, I was afraid....' Her voice trailed away. 'I'm glad I came back now. And I'll try Mrs. Harrison, as you suggest.

168

What number is her house?'

Mrs. Harrison was a tall gaunt-looking woman in her late fifties, with greying brown hair and piercing grey eyes, the complete antithesis of the jolly, plump English landlady, in fact, and yet Debra perceived humour in the bright eyes, and intelligence in the firm lines of her forehead. She agreed that she had taken in paying guests, and to Debra's relief had a vacant room at the moment.

'Two weeks' rent in advance,' she said, smiling at the girl. 'I provide breakfast and evening dinner, you provide your own lunch, except on Sundays.'

'That sounds fine,' murmured Debra, handing over the necessary notes. 'And this room is quite delightful.'

And so it was, with chintz curtains and bedspread, and a warm pink carpet covering the floor. The view was rather less inspiring, with a brick wall giving on to a stretch of concrete that backed some shops, but that didn't matter, she thought, sinking down on to the bed wearily. She was here, and had her job back, and all without anyone's assistance.

Later she viewed the precarious state of her finances. If she lived frugally she should be able to last until September. But there would be nothing left for luxuries, and smoking was definitely *out*.

As though to make up to her for everything the weather became almost perfect for the remainder of the month. The skies were a cerulean blue and the sun shone every day. Debra made friends with the Harrison's teenage son Nicholas, and he accompanied her almost everywhere she went once school was over. He had a transistor radio and most often they would be found down on the river bank, sitting talking, while Nicholas cast his fishing rod lazily into the clear water. Nicholas was fifteen, and Debra got to know everything about him, from his favourite pop stars to his secret ambition to become a writer. He wrote short stories, and some poetry, and Debra loved to lie on the river bank just listening to him reading his latest composition to her while the transistor provided a thought-chasing background.

A week after she arrived back in Valleydown she found herself in the area leading to River Walk, and with reluctant steps she walked along the opposite side of the street to her aunt's house, glancing surreptitiously across at the net-curtained windows. The place looked deserted, and she frowned and crossed the road, tempted to ring the bell to ascertain whether her aunt was at home or not.

Then fussy little Mrs. Mannering who lived next door came bustling out. Debra had always said that nothing ever happened in River Walk without Mrs. Mannering being acutely aware of it. She greeted Debra with curious eyes, and said: 'If you're looking for your aunt, she's not there.'

Debra was about to say that she was certainly not looking for her aunt when something about Mrs. Mannering's suppressedly excited attitude caused her to say casually: 'Isn't she? Where is she?'

'Don't you know?' Mrs. Mannering folded her arms with some satisfaction and it was obvious she had plenty to relate. Debra, despising herself for her curiosity, lifted her shoulders helplessly.

'If I knew I wouldn't be asking,' she said.

Mrs. Mannering studied her deliberately. 'Well, she's gone away. To Italy, so I hear.'

'*Italy?*'

'Yes, Italy. For a holiday. At least, that's where she's starting from. She'll very likely go on from there.'

'But——' Debra shook her head. 'I mean—I see!' She bit her lip. She could hardly tell Mrs. Mannering that her aunt had never had any money to do that sort of thing. But Mrs. Mannering must have guessed, because she said: 'She won a competition. That's how she could afford it.'

'A competition?' Debra felt she was being completely stupid echoing everything Mrs. Mannering said, but her aunt had never been the kind of person who entered competitions.

'Yes. She won several thousand pounds, I believe. On the pools, most likely.'

'The pools?' Again Debra felt flabbergasted. 'I see. Do you know when she'll be back?'

'No. But not for some time, I don't think. She left the house key with me.'

'With you?' Debra shook her head bewilderedly. It simply was not like Aunt Julia to leave the house key with anyone.

Mrs. Mannering ran a tongue over her thick lips. 'Do you want to go in?'

'No. That is ...., Debra hesitated. Wouldn't now be an ideal opportunity to collect all the little bits of things of hers which she had so badly not wanted to lose? 'I—would you mind?' she asked awkwardly.

'Course not. It's your home, isn't it?' Mrs. Mannering frowned, and Debra thought with relief that at least she did not know what had happened in America. 'I thought you was in America, some place,' she said, continuing. 'Your aunt didn't expect you back, did she?'

'No. No, she didn't,' said Debra truthfully. 'Er—could I have that key, Mrs. Mannering?'

'All right. Do you want to come in a minute and have a cup of tea?'

'No, thank you. I—I just want to collect some books,' said Debra, shivering a little.

'All right.' Mrs. Mannering gave her another studied glance, and then turning, walked into her own

171

house.

The key turned smoothly in the lock, and Debra stepped inside, dropping the latch behind her. She had no desire for Mrs. Mannering to come peering after her, wondering what she was up to. She felt like an intruder as it was, and she quelled the feeling of fear the surroundings bred in her. She could remember the last time she had been in this house so well.

She walked down the passage into the living room. Everywhere smelt damp and shuttered, and she wonderd how long it was since her aunt went away. Dust lay thickly on everything, so it must have been some time ago.

Leaving downstairs, she went up to her room, and began to gather together her small store of personal things; books, letters from school friends and college associates, several small ornaments and a suitcase containing sentimental things like school reports and exercise books, and one or two little mementoes of holidays spent on the coast. The small case was half empty, so she squashed the other things into it and fastened the lid tightly. Then she emerged on to the landing again. Standing down her case, she looked into her aunt's severe bedroom. It had always had a masculine air, and was always immaculately clean and tidy. But now a piece of paper lay uncharacteristically in the middle of the floor, and as Debra bent automatically to pick it up she saw an old brown suitcase protruding from under her aunt's bed. Barely glancing at the paper, she pulled out the case and was about to thrust the letter inside when the sight of an envelope bearing an enormous American stamp caught her eye.

She sat on her haunches, the letter in her hand, staring at the postmark: *Los Angeles*! The date stamped on it was the twelfth of February, 1971. Debra felt her heart thumping loudly. It could be a coincidence, or it could not. With trembling fingers she turned over the letter in her hand. It was a bank statement, dated some seven months previously. It was in her aunt's name and revealed that at that time her aunt had a bank balance of eight thousand five hundred pounds, and some odd pence. Debra sat back on her heels, aghast. There must be some mistake. Her aunt had never had more than her pension. She could not possibly have saved that amount of money. Besides, she had always taken almost all of Debra's salary to help support them because they had so little

Debra bit her lip hard, trying to quell the tightness in her chest, the apprehensive feeling of impending disaster. She studied the statement dispassionately. It was all there, the tiny withdrawals made throughout the previous year, and the large amount of interest accrued.

Debra put the statement into the case and picked up the letter, turning it over in her hand with shaking fingers. Then with decision she opened it and extracted the letter. The letter began *Dear Julia*, and when she turned to the end she read *Yours, Elizabeth*. The room swam round her for a moment, and then, as the giddiness passed, she began to read with painstaking care.

At the end of the letter she sank down on to the floor feeling an overwhelming sense of loss. This might be the only letter of her mother's that she might read, and its simplicity revealed more potently than words could ever say how much her mother had regretted her hasty decision to leave Debra with her sister. She asked innumerable questions about her, about her health and her school work, about her friends and her appearance. And the most important thing from Debra's point of view was the mention of the cheque that Elizabeth was enclosing. From the gist of its inclusion it was obvious that Elizabeth had been sending money to Julia for her child's support, and this was how Julia had amassed such a bank balance. This was only one of the letters, and Debra wondered shakily how much Elizabeth had been obliged to send.

Putting aside her normal respect for her aunt's possessions, she searched feverishly through the papers in the case, and finally came upon the thing she sought: her aunt's bank book. She opened it, ran a finger down the list of entries, and then gave a heavy sigh. Julia had been receiving two hundred and fifty dollars a month for as far back as the book was dated.

With blank depression, she replaced everything in the small case, and sliding it back under the bed got to her feet. She walked unsteadily to the door, leaning against it feeling really sick now. No pools win for Julia, but the result of careful saving for years past. How unfortunate for her that Elizabeth was killed, Debra thought cynically, wondering why her aunt had waited until now to spend the money. Unless, by keeping the money a secret, she had achieved that which she most desired: the means to keep Debra tied to her, both financially as well as physically. And now Debra knew the truth, and Julia was free to do what she liked at last.

Debra staggered into the bathroom and leaned weakly over the basin. She had thought that nothing more could happen to her. *How wrong could you be!*

As she lay there, trying to hold on to her emotions, the door bell rang. She straightened up, wiping her face with a towel. She would not answer it. No one knew she was here. Yes, Mrs. Mannering knew she was here. She would wonder why Debra did not answer the door if she ignored it. She might even come looking for her. She *couldn't* face Mrs. Mannering just now.

She went shakily down the stairs and into the small

hall. She unlatched the door and opened it. Then she stepped back aghast, as Aaron stepped into the doorway. He saw the pale cheeks, the terrible torment in her eyes, and closing the door gathered her into his arms. It was like coming home, and Debra clung to him convulsively. Aaron did not say anything. For the moment, actions were enough.

CHAPTER NINE

AN hour later Debra and Aaron were sitting in the lounge of the Crown Hotel in Valleydown market place. It was deserted at this hour of the day, and they could talk freely. In brief, stilted sentences Debra had told Aaron about the things she had accidentally stumbled upon that afternoon, and he had listened without interruption, merely nodding now and then when Debra halted nervously. He had not yet mentioned his own reasons for being here, but Debra was too relieved to see him to care.

At last she said: 'So that's that. At least now I don't feel any sense of obligation towards her for looking after me. Oh, Aaron, why did she do it? Why couldn't she have been *human*! I mean—we're all human, aren't we?'

Aaron half-smiled, lighting a cigar. 'Yes, we're all human.' He patted her hand. 'And now, we have much to talk about that concerns no one but ourselves. Why did you run away from me, Debra? Why did you do that?'

Debra swallowed hard. 'Didn't—didn't Dominic McGill tell you?'

'A little. A little. But I want to hear it from you.'

'Well, surely you have your suspicions.' Debra twisted her hands. 'After all, you told me to beware of McGill yourself.'

'So I did. But that was before....' He stopped. 'Anyway, that couldn't have been all of it. I can't believe that you would run away from Dominic without telling me the reason why. There was something more, wasn't there? Come on, you might as well tell me. I mean to know.'

Debra shook her head. 'Didn't Dominic tell you that, too?'

'As a matter of fact he did.'

'What!'

'Yes. Some story Marsha Mathews had seen fit to regale you with. Am I right?'

Debra stared at him. 'He told you?'

'Why not? We're friends, Dominic and I, we don't lie to one another.'

'And you believe that?' Debra's eyes were wide.

Aaron's face darkened with anger. 'Debra, don't belittle our relationship. Nothing you've heard has any bearing on the truth. Only you're too small a person to understand, it seems. You were willing to take the word of a woman like Marsha Mathews rather than ask me and discover the real truth.'

Debra's cheeks burned. 'I don't know what you mean,' she said dully.

'Apparently not.' His expression softened. 'Oh, Debra my dear, you've had enough to bear today, I won't berate you for your carelessness. But it seems the time has come to tell you a little about Dominic and your mother.'

Debra looked up. 'You know about them?'

'Yes, I know. But not what you imagine there is to know. Debra, why are you so willing to believe the worst of Dominic? Has he ever done anything to hurt you?'

'No, but—well, is it true that he went with Elizabeth to the Philippines, just two weeks after his play was accepted?'

'Yes, it's true. But they weren't alone, if that's what you mean. I went as well.'

'You?'

'Of course. It was a holiday, I freely admit, but we

did take the cameras, and we did some filming for a new movie. Exterior shots, and so on. Nothing tiring or energetic.'

'I see.' Debra bent her head. 'Go on.'

Aaron studied her downbent head. 'And will you listen with a slightly more open mind now?' he asked.

She sighed and nodded.

'Good. Then I'll begin at the beginning, shall I? How much do you know of Dom's early background?'

'I know what Victor told me. About living in New York, and that's about all.'

'I see. Well, when he wrote "Avenida" I was in New York. Elizabeth was appearing in a play on Broadway, and she was already moderately successful. Dominic had already been the rounds of the agents with this play, but in his position—he was working as a barman at that time, with practically no money to his name— he hadn't a chance, and he knew it.' He smiled. 'But perhaps knowing Dom as you do you'll realise that that was not the final answer. He knew that where Elizabeth was to be found, there also would I be. So he waylaid us on the way to the theatre one evening, and practically-thrust the play into my face. I was pretty mad, I can tell you. I was used to theatre-crazy writers trying to make a fast buck. But Dom was something else again. Elizabeth saw him, and she liked what she saw. Why not? He was a mighty attractive guy, and obviously it wasn't simply his play that she was interested in.'

Debra's cheeks burned afresh, and she looked at Aaron. 'Didn't you care?'

'About what? Elizabeth liked men around. That wasn't to say she had affairs with every man she met. Besides, Dom was too young for her. Even though he was years older than his age in experience. Anyway, she persuaded me to read the play, and finally, because

I loved Elizabeth, I did just that.' He drew on his cigar. 'It was then that I realised that Dom's was no ordinary talent. He has an aptitude for situations rarely found in screen writers, and "Avenida" was obviously a gem of a part for Elizabeth, at least the part of Laura was. So we told him we liked his play, and we gave him an advance which he promptly blew in on a Mercedes sports with an engine he himself tuned to capacity.' He chuckled. 'Crazy idiot!' He said it with a warmth of feeling that Debra responded to. 'We were planning this trip to Fiji. Elizabeth wanted him along. She said he could study screen writing first-hand while we were away. I knew she wanted his company, so I agreed. That was how he came along.' He sighed. 'I freely admit, Debra, that Elizabeth wanted Dominic, but unfortunately Dominic just wasn't interested. Man, can't you understand, he was a young and attractive male, used to adoration from beautiful girls, even if moneywise they weren't in Elizabeth's class, and even for the sake of his writing he wasn't prepared to be any older woman's plaything. Elizabeth suffered terribly at first. You see, no matter what your aunt may have told you, she was not as hard as she liked to make out, and she could be *hurt*.'

Debra clasped her fingers tightly, recalling something Dominic had once said, something about Elizabeth being able to be hurt, *unfortunately*. Was that what he had meant?

Aaron studied her expression. 'Don't you see, Debra, that the reason Dominic didn't tell you all this was not because he was afraid it might come to my ears, but because he respected your mother, he was even fond of her in a purely unsexual way, and he knew if he told you how she used to run after him, you would have despised her, and hated him for destroying any illusions you might hold.'

Debra pressed the palms of her hands to her cheeks. 'Marsha Mathews was so positive!'

'Yes, but more than that, you were prepared to believe her, because that was what you wanted to believe,' exclaimed Aaron fiercely. 'For so long this aunt of yours has destroyed any natural feelings that you think everyone is alike.'

'Oh, Aaron!'

'Well, it's true. From the very beginning you were prepared to believe the worst about your mother, and when Dominic showed any interest in you, you immediately thought he was using you as a substitute for your mother. Isn't that right?'

'I suppose so.' Debra bit her lip until it bled.

'Why? Because you realised you were falling in love with Dominic yourself, and you used this—this relationship to develop in your mind into a sordid and terrible thing. Oh, Debra! Can't you see how wrong you were? I swear to you that Dominic was never your mother's lover, no matter how much she might have wanted it!'

Debra hunched her shoulders. 'Tell me about this crash he had,' she said. 'When was that?'

'It happened exactly twenty-four hours after your mother was killed in the plane crash,' muttered Aaron, his eyes sombre now. 'Elizabeth hadn't wanted to go to New York to take part in this festival, and Dominic persuaded her. She was flying from Los Angeles to New York when the crash occurred. There were no survivors. The wreck was completely burned out. Dominic naturally blamed himself for her being on that particular flight. He himself took her to the airport. The day after he took the Porsche out on the freeway, and let it have its head. He expected, he *wanted* to crash, and he did. It's as simple as that.' Aaron sighed. 'Fortunately he was not killed. By the

180

time he had recovered he had seen so much genuine misery that he had no more desire to be among it. He realised he had behaved stupidly and childishly. I guess you could say we helped one another to get over it.'

'I see. You make me feel very small.'

'Only very young, and very inexperienced,' replied Aaron, more kindly. 'What are you going to do now?'

Debra shook her head. 'How did you find me?'

'Quite easily. I naturally assumed you would go to your aunt's to live again. I called there simply because that was where I expected to find you. But you haven't answered my question. What are you going to do now?'

'I don't know. I really don't know.'

'Don't you? Don't you really want to go back to the States, to see Dominic? For God's sake, Debra, be honest with yourself for once. Isn't that really what you want?'

Debra stared at him with tearful eyes. 'And if it is?'

'Then come back with me.'

'But I mean—oh, Aaron, I couldn't work with Dominic, really I couldn't. Feeling the way I do, it would be disastrous! I wouldn't be able to resist him if he really wanted me. I'm sorry, Aaron, but you asked me to be honest, and I am.'

Aaron studied the glowing tip of his cigar. 'All right, don't work with him, then. Don't make the film.'

'But you wanted me to.'

'It's not a matter of life and death. Your happiness is more important to me than the film.'

'Is it? Is it really?' Debra smiled tremulously. 'Aaron, I don't know what to say.'

'Say you'll come with me,' he pleaded earnestly. 'Please, Debra. Don't let me down.'

'I've just arranged with Miss Gantry at the school that I should resume my teaching duties in September,' murmured Debra thoughtfully.

'I'll see this Miss Gantry myself if that's all that's troubling you.' Aaron looked at her questioningly. 'Well?'

Debra hesitated only a moment longer. 'All right, I'll come.'

'And this time it's for keeps,' said Aaron firmly. 'I won't let you run away again.'

Debra rolled over in bed, then sat up, blinking at the bright sunlight that penetrated the half-open venetian blinds at her window. For a moment she wondered where she was, then it all came flooding back to her. She was in her room in Aaron's house, deep in the heart of Los Angeles. They had arrived late the previous evening, and she had gone straight to bed, putting on the filmy nightdress, only one of many, which lined the closet drawers here in her room. In the sliding wardrobe were all the beautiful dresses Aaron had brought for her, and outside those windows stretched the sweet-scented gardens of the rambling house. She felt happy, with a deep sense of contentment, which she refused to acknowledge had anything to do with Dominic McGill. And yet it was overwhelmingly sweet to know that any attraction he felt for her was not because she looked like her mother.

She slid out of bed and dressed in slim-fitting slacks of a mustard-coloured nylon, and a loose yellow overblouse that had ruffles at the neckline and wrists. She left her heavy hair loose and straight, and walked down to breakfast with Aaron.

Aaron smiled appreciatively at her. 'I certainly have missed your company these last few mornings,' he said. 'You brighten up the breakfast table considerably.'

Debra smiled in return. 'What are you doing to-day?'

'I have to go to the studios this morning, and this afternoon I have a conference. What are you going to do?'

'I don't know.' She shrugged her slim shoulders. 'Could I come to the studios with you?'

Aaron's eyes widened. 'Why, I guess you could at that. But Dominic will be there.'

'That's—that's all right. I have to meet him sooner or later, so I might as well get it over with.'

'True enough. All right, Debra, we leave in half an hour.'

The Alpha Film Studios occupied several acres of land outside of town. They were not half so glamorous as her ideas of a film studio, even though there were the inevitable lines of stages, with mock-ups of towns and villages, saloons and theatres. Aaron left her in the charge of a young woman called Millie McAndrew who showed her round, and indicated the various techniques relevant to film producing. It was all amazingly compact, and Debra lost her nervousness in her intense interest of what was going on. Galleries, built above ground level, contained offices and rooms for the writers to work in, and there were photographic studios and developing rooms, and all the basic machinery for film cutting.

Later in the morning, Debra was returned to Aaron, and they had coffee together in his office. It was while they were drinking the delicious coffee and smoking cigarettes that the door opened to admit Dominic, accompanied by a slim blonde girl, dressed in slacks and a chunky sweater, her hair caught up in a pony-tail. Debra seemed to shrink within herself, and it took a great deal of courage to look up at him and answer his perfunctory greeting.

'This is Diana Linden,' said Aaron, nodding to the girl with Dominic. 'She's Dom's secretary——'

'And general dogsbody,' interrupted the girl good-humouredly. 'You must be Debra Warren, Aaron's daughter.'

'That's right,' Debra nodded, overwhelmingly conscious of Dominic's cold eyes watching her. When she had looked at him she had seen the cold distasteful look upon his face and it made something inside her curl up and die.

'And how have you settled down?' asked Diana interestedly. 'I expect you find it all quite alarming after England.' She grinned up at Dominic with dancing eyes. 'After all, you have the two most personable men in Hollywood running around after you, and that's really something!' she laughed.

Debra tried to act naturally, but all she could do was smile rather stiffly, and acknowledge the other girl's friendly overtures. Dominic spoke with Aaron, then without speaking to Debra again, he put an arm round Diana's shoulders and said: 'Come on, slave-driver, we have plenty to do.'

After they had gone, Aaron looked across at Debra. 'Well,' he said, 'what did you expect?' He breathed hard down his nose. 'Dominic's his own man. He won't run around after anyone. Least of all someone he—well, who treated him like you did.'

Debra sighed, 'I think I'd like to go home, Aaron. I don't want to meet him again.'

Coward, said a small voice inside her, but she ignored it.

Aaron shrugged his shoulders, but lifted the telephone, and a few minutes later the car was waiting for her to go home. A week passed by during which time she saw Dominic on three separate occasions, and each time was treated with the same kind of cold indifference he had exhibited on that first occasion. Debra tried not to care, but it was much too difficult for her, seeing him, and knowing he hated and despised her.

At last she came to a decision. *She* would have to go to him; tell him that she knew she had been wrong about him now, and ask him to accept her apology. It seemed a forlorn hope; she had misjudged him too many times before.

Not mentioning her decision to Aaron, she rang Dominic's house late one afternoon when she knew he would be home. Aaron was still at the studios, but he had told Debra that Dominic was working at home on the new script. One of the servants answered, and when she asked to speak to Dominic they came back with the message that he was in conference and not to be disturbed. She didn't believe it. She was convinced he was merely ignoring her and she slammed down the receiver, staring moodily at it.

Finally she changed into a slim-fitting sheath of apricot tricel and ordered the car. The chauffeur was surprised when she gave him Dominic's address, but said nothing. The traffic was terrific at this time of day, thousands of vehicles converging on the intersections, and the fumes and the sounds of car klaxons rang in her ears. She was nervous, tense and uncertain, but if she had not come at once she would never have been able to summon up her courage again.

The ocean looked incredibly cool and beautiful, and once inside the high wall surrounding Dominic's house the sounds of the day faded into obscurity. As she stepped out of the car she looked down on the stretch of beach longingly. It was all so clean and fresh and magnificent. Whatever happened she would never forget this place.

She walked through the courtyard tentatively, leaving the chauffeur staring after her curiously. The fountain sounded refreshing and she sighed. Looking about her, she had no idea where she might find Dominic. She had no idea where his study might be, even though she had been there twice. It was so vast, and she felt she could lose herself in its corridors.

A sound behind her brought her round to face the manservant she had seen the night Dominic carried her up from the beach, Joseph.

'Yes, miss?' he said questioningly.

'Oh! I—er—I rang Mr. McGill earlier, but I was told he was in conference. It's most urgent that I see him. . . .'

'Mr. McGill *was* in conference,' said Joseph politely. 'A Mr. Lindsay Harrigan was here earlier. He left a few minutes ago.'

'I see.' So she had been wrong again. She felt mean and malicious. No wonder Dominic despised her!

'Then—then could I see Mr. McGill, *please*?'

Joseph bowed his head. 'I'll see if he is available,' he nodded calmly, and turned, but then halted abruptly as Dominic came walking lazily out of the arched entrance to the hall. 'Oh, Mr. Dominic, this young lady would like to speak with you.'

'Thank you, Joseph.' Dominic indicated that the servant should leave them. Then he looked at Debra. 'Yes? What do you want?'

Debra clasped her hands together tightly, completely at a loss for words for a moment. He looked so dear and familiar, and she registered everything about him in that first moment: the short ruffled silvery hair, the dark-lashed blue eyes, and his lean hard body dressed in close-fitting dark pants and a round-necked navy blue sweater.

'I—I want to talk to you,' she said awkwardly.

'What about?' His voice was cold.

'Oh, can't we go inside? I don't like talking out here

186

where anyone can hear us.'

'Surely what we have to say to one another isn't worth the trouble of entering the building,' he remarked sardonically. 'What have you come for? Some errand from Aaron?'

'No,' Debra rubbed her elbows with the palms of her hands. 'Please, Dominic, don't be like this. I came to say—I was sorry.'

'*Sorry?*' He stared at her with narrowed eyes. 'I see. And what am I supposed to say to that?'

Debra bent her head. 'Maybe that you accept my apology.'

'Why should I do that? Why should I give you that satisfaction? I owe you nothing, but *nothing*!'

'I know that. I have been stupid,' she said 'Look, I know you have every right to be mad at me, but try and see it from my viewpoint. After all, all I know of my mother is hearsay. What was I expected to understand? That she was a beautiful woman, sweet and charming, kind and generous, a woman it must have been easy for a man to love——'

'But not *me*!' he interrupted her.

'But it wasn't unreasonable that I should think that,' she pleaded. 'You knew her so well. Can't you try to understand?

'Why should I? What's it to you what I believe?'

'Can't you see? I've been small-minded and an idiot! What more can I say?' She turned away, her voice breaking uncontrollably.

She felt him close behind her suddenly, and his breath fanned her neck. His fingers curved round her throat almost threateningly. She held her breath for a long moment, and he said: 'So all right, I accept your apology.' He allowed his hands to fall to his sides. 'You can go. You've exonerated yourself.'

Debra moved away jerkily towards the fountain,

allowing her fingers to trail in its cooling shower. Her hair fell forward, hiding her expression, and Dominic said harshly: 'For God's sake, Debra, go!'

She straightened, her back still to him as she spoke. 'Aaron told me how you got your back injury. Obviously carrying me up from the beach was responsible for its being strained. I'm sorry. Is it—is it all right now?'

'Perfectly.' His voice was still cool.

She turned and looked at him desperately. 'Tell me, the reason you followed me to London—was it all to do with Aaron?'

He shrugged. 'Does it matter?'

'Of course it matters.' She compressed her lips. 'I want to know.'

'It hasn't troubled you for the last two weeks. Why should it trouble you now?'

'You don't know that. You only think you do,' she said unsteadily. 'Of course I wanted to know. Even in London—even when I thought you and my mother were—well—I still needed to know. But you left. You didn't even try to defend yourself. Why didn't you?'

He moved his shoulders carelessly. 'I don't intend to explain my actions. If you can't accept me as you find me then it mustn't matter.'

'I don't understand.'

His voice hardened. 'On the contrary; I think you understand me very well. Maybe it amuses you to play around with a man's emotions, but I can assure you it doesn't amuse me.'

Debra stared at him in astonishment. 'No, honestly, Dominic, I don't know what you mean.'

'Oh, don't give me that!' he muttered savagely. 'You've known for some time the effect you can produce on *me*!' His tone was violent. 'Don't think I haven't fought it, because I have, but you've deliberately attempted to make me dance to your pretty little tune. Well, this time you went too far. I've had it. Up to here.' He raised his hand to his chin.

'*Dominic!*' She stared at him uncomprehendingly. '*Please*, don't be like this.' She closed her eyes for a moment, still unable to accept what he had said. 'You —you like a lot of women. You said so yourself. Or Aaron did, I don't remember! Me, I'm just someone who accidentally got thrown into the scene. You've never given me any indication that I meant anything to you!'

'Haven't I? Good God!' He raised his eyes heavenward. 'Ask anyone you care to mention and you'll find that I never pursue a woman, they pursue me.' This was said without any sense of conceit. 'I guess money talks, like it always did. But you!—You were different. I guess at first it was your resemblance to Elizabeth, but later....' He stopped. 'Anyway, like I said, this is the parting of the ways. I won't get in your hair, if you'll not get in mine.'

'*Dominic!*' she repeated. 'Stop talking, *please*.' She stared at him, her eyes wide and disbelieving, even now.

Dominic's eyes narrowed. 'If I stop talking things might get out of hand,' he said, in a taut voice. Then he turned and walked away towards the house without looking at her again.

Debra hesitated only a moment, then she followed him. He walked into the ballroom, empty now, its crystal chandeliers with hanging prisms tinkling like windflowers in the gentle breeze. Debra stopped, turning round, taking in everything she saw with an increased sense of perception. Dominic had stopped in the middle of the dance floor, watching her, his eyes intent. Debra halted too, feeling strangely nervous suddenly.

'Your car is waiting for you,' he said huskily.

'I know it.'

'Then go take it home.'

'It depends where one calls home,' she murmured softly.

Dominic's eyes narrowed disturbingly. 'What does that mean? Debra, I warn you, don't play with me, or you may get more than you bargained for.'

Debra half-smiled and then spread wide her hands, whirling round as she did so. 'This is a marvellous place,' she said rapturously. 'Even in daylight it has a magic all its own.'

Dominic stiffened, his fists clenched. 'Look,' he said, in a low tone, 'I'm tired. I've been working since early this morning. I've no time for your childishness.' His words were deliberately hurtful.

But Debra merely stopped smiling and walked towards him slowly, holding her eyes with his. As she neared him, he held out a hand grasping her wrist painfully. 'You're crazy,' he groaned achingly. 'Debra, if you don't mean this, you're *crazy!*'

'Oh, but I do mean it,' she said softly, twisting her wrist out of his hold and moving closer to him. 'Yes, you do look tired.' She traced the lines of his cheek with the tips of her fingers.

He caught her hand, pressing his mouth with warm insistence to the palm, and Debra shivered with delicious anticipation, winding her arms round his neck, twisting her fingers in his hair, drawing his mouth down to hers. For several minutes there was silence in the ballroom, then Dominic asserted himself, and pushed her slightly back in the circle of his arms, looking at her seriously.

'Debra,' he muttered, 'don't make any mistake, this is for real with me. If you live with me, it's for all time. I know I'm too old for you,' and then: 'Yes, I am,' as she pressed her fingers against his lips, 'but God help me, I can't let you go!'

'What do you mean, *live with you*?' she asked, with smiling eyes.

'You know what I mean,' he muttered. 'It means I want to marry you.'

'Dominic!' She held his face between the palms of her hands. '*Why?* Tell me why?'

'Because I love you, I need you, I can't live without you.' He kissed the side of her neck. 'Don't you think that's some admission?' He smiled wryly. 'I never believed I would ever say those words. But you, with your quaint little ideas, somehow twined yourself about me so that I can think of nothing else. You asked me why I followed you to London—I'll tell you. Because I was nearly off my head with worry,' he buried his face in her hair. 'Oh, lord, Debra, marry me soon, but *soon*. I want you.' His mouth found hers, and Debra returned his kiss with all the fervour of her untried youth. It didn't matter now about anything that had gone before. It was the future that mattered, and maybe Elizabeth could see them and be glad that Dominic loved her daughter.

One of the best things in life is ... FREE

We're sure you have enjoyed this Mills & Boon romance. So we'd like you to know about the other titles we offer. A world of variety in romance. From the best authors in the world of romance.

The Mills & Boon Reader Service Catalogue lists all the romances that are currently in stock. So if there are any titles that you cannot obtain or have missed in the past, you can get the romances you want DELIVERED DIRECT to your home.

The Reader Service Catalogue is free. Simply send the coupon – or drop us a line asking for the catalogue.

Post to: Mills & Boon Reader Service, P.O. Box 236, Thornton Road, Croydon, Surrey CR9 3RU, England.
*Please note: READERS IN SOUTH AFRICA please write to: Mills & Boon Ltd., P.O. Box 1872, Johannesburg 2000, S. Africa.

Please send me my FREE copy of the Mills & Boon Reader Service Catalogue.

NAME (Mrs/Miss)_____ EP1

ADDRESS_____

COUNTY/COUNTRY_____ POST/ZIP CODE_____
BLOCK LETTERS, PLEASE

Mills & Boon
the rose of romance